shines a light with empathy onto small lives lived humbly on the margins." — Max Weiss, Professor of History and Near Eastern Studies, Princeton University and author of *In the Shadow of Sectarianism: Law, Shi'ism and the Making of Modern Lebanon*

The Penguin's Song

The Penguin's Song

Hassan Daoud

Translated from the Arabic by Marilyn Booth

City Lights Books | San Francisco

Library of Congress Cataloging-in-Publication Data
Dawud, Hasan.
 [Ghina' al-batriq. English]
 The penguin's song / Hassan Daoud ; translated from the Arabic by
Marilyn Booth. – First City Lights Books edition
   pages cm
 ISBN 978-0-87286-623-2
 I. Booth, Marilyn, translator. II. Title.

 PJ7820.A8425G5513 2014
 892.7'36–dc23

                    2014024970

City Lights Books are published at the City Lights Bookstore
261 Columbus Avenue, San Francisco, CA 94133
www.citylights.com

MIX
Paper from
responsible sources
FSC® C011935

The Penguin's Song

I

FROM OUR HOME ON THE building's third and upper-most floor, from its balcony and through its windows, I can observe the entire breadth of the city below me. The others who live in our district—but in buildings that only begin to rise up where the unpaved sand track ends (or where it begins, if we're heading toward where we live, at its very end)—can-not see the city as we do. Over there, the apartments face each other closely; and unlike ours, their buildings do not sit on a rise. The congestion that suddenly clogs the street where their buildings begin draws even the residents of the higher floors, who might be able to glimpse something of the city, to engross themselves instead with what is happening directly below them on the street. How dense the crowds are over there! We can see all of that commotion from our own bedroom win-dows, but the noise of it doesn't reach us. When we're walking on the sand track, coming back toward the building where we live, those sounds reverberate in our bodies, even as they fade away behind us with every step. By the time we're get-ting close to our building all we can hear is the sound of the wind coming up from below. It's as if all that separates us from those people over there is the unpaved distance we must walk on the sand; we are their hinterland, inhabiting a countryside they never enter, accessed by a path they never walk. They can't even change its aspect over time, by building over here, for instance. That's because of land inheritance issues. My father knows all about the reasons for that.

So our old building stands alone here, a mere three floors rising on the knoll like a short, fat tower. From the kitchen window and the window in one of the bedrooms, and also from the roomy balcony off the sitting room, I can see the whole city at one glance, massed together in a single tight clump, as if ringed by an invisible band out there on that flat expanse. In the days after we first moved in, my father would sketch circles in the air with his finger, the first one enclosing nearly half the city and then each ring growing slightly smaller, one circle sketched within another, until finally at the end of this little exercise he could say that his shop was exactly *there*. There it is, that's the one, right there! he would say to my mother as he pulled her closer to his rigidly outstretched arm, his index finger forming an extension, completing the straight line as he pointed precisely at his target. Come here, you, he would say to me when he saw her gaze straying to shift among objects she could not make out clearly. Look, son, he would say. Isn't that our shop? You—you know our shop. . . .

Yes, I know our shop. But I did not like being there, sitting in that shop as my father made me do. He would plant me in his chair, which sat in the only unoccupied space in the shop, a small and cramped bit of emptiness. I faced the street with my back to the huge jute sacks, open with their top edges rolled back to reveal the goods inside. My father thought I found it entertaining to watch the passersby making their slow and cautious way along the narrow street paved with ancient stone blocks, wary of slipping into the grimy, mucky gutter running down the middle of it. It would never have occurred to my father that they were entertaining themselves with me, but that's the way I saw it. After all, they were the ones who, peering into the shop, could stare at me, at my body facing out from the storefront that opened directly onto the street.

I didn't like my father's way of working in the shop, either. His sprightly movements and winning gestures seemed inappropriate for his age. To me, he always gave the impression of being caught up in a trade war, constantly trying to get an edge on some competitor who might steal away his profits. Whenever one of those customers who know their way around the shops came in, I would tell myself that perhaps now my father would at least show a little embarrassment at my having to see him act this way. Making a sale—he would say to me—means having to put on a show for the customer. It was as if he wanted to apologize for his spryness, for the charming insistence that infected both gestures and speech as he played up to these shoppers. He never asked me to help him. Sometimes I would give him an inquisitive look to show him that I was ready to join in, but he never accepted my assistance.

After our move here, though, which was thirteen years ago, my father would leave home only to take his walk, which didn't formally begin (as he saw it) until he had put the sand track behind him and reached those buildings. What seemed to direct his steps was the aim of finding out which shops were open, and to see whether he recognized them or knew their owners from back in the days when he had worked in his own shop. In that year when the old city was being emptied and all its shops closed, one after another of the merchants who had been there began to open up other shops in various quarters as replacements for their old establishments. In these new locations, though, the shops no longer formed a single, connected, impenetrable row, sitting practically on top of each other as they had in the old city. My father, as keen as he was to make a daily tally of their number, had to walk to the very end of each cluster of buildings to find them. Indeed, he had to regularly monitor buildings that he had already scouted on earlier excursions, since the shops changed hands often and the ways in which these spaces were used also seemed to be in constant flux.

Whenever my mother remarked that he would be better off opening a shop and working rather than frittering away his time with walking, he would respond by saying, for instance, that Makkawi, who had made the tastiest stewed fuul beans in Maarad, in the old city's center, had had to open his new eatery in a tiny niche tucked into the entryway of some building. Or that Uwayni, whose merchandise had filled three entire floors up to the ceilings, was now stuffed into a tiny, cramped, out-of-the-way refuge that had to hold not only all of his goods, but his employees as well.

It's all temporary, my mother would answer. Temporary! She didn't have to wait very long to hear him bark that he would never work in a shop in some stairwell, whether it was temporary or forever. And when he finished by saying that he would rather stay as he was, keeping his dignity even if it meant not working, I would wonder if he wasn't overdoing the respect he owed his old shop. After all, it had been a small, constricted space beneath a ceiling that bore down severely on the interior, hunching over it like a heavy, oversize ribbed vault; the entire breadth of the shop, moreover, was open to the narrow, grimy lane. In the hours I spent sitting there, on that chair among the huge sacks, I mostly stared at my surroundings wondering what someone else—someone my age but with a sound body—would make of my situation, of this place, of me sitting mutely on the chair as I always did. I could not find anything pleasing about any of it—not my father nor the huge open sacks nor the floor permeated by a grime that had altered its original color before creeping across it to add a layer of filth. Sitting there, I would imagine myself keeping back that filth, scraping it off with one of those enormous old wooden-handled iron knives.

It was an old place, with the kind of oldness about it that makes it seem automatically unclean. The sort of ancientness that means the ceiling and walls are so rough and thick and heavy that they appear strong when they are actually fragile to the point of crumbling, could actually collapse as you're looking at them. Look . . . look there, look at it, my father says to me. He has given up on my mother and brings me close, his arm jutting out straight as an arrow, his rigid finger pointing. When I seem to be looking where he wants me to look, craning my head forward to comply, I don't see the façade. What I see is the shop from the inside, emptied of its goods. But its smell remains, alive and pungent, filling the space even if no one is there to smell it.

You know it . . . you do know where it is, over there, don't you? He asks me this so that I can't help but acknowledge that he remembers it. Here and now, from this apartment, he remembers it all, and he remembers being there. Insisting that we are actually seeing his shop, even when we are as far away as this, he can let himself believe that someone else sees the same picture. Someone else remembers along with him. He finds it hard to sustain that memory alone; he doesn't feel entirely comfortable or certain about it. You could have read all those books of yours, he says to me, reminding me that he thinks I wasted a lot of good hours that I could have put to good use. If only I had spent all those hours sitting in his shop with a book in my hands. But with my miniature hands and arms, I would have had to stick them out in front of me as far as I possibly could to be able to read the words. And then those people walking down the lane and peering into the shop could entertain themselves even better, since they wouldn't have to limit themselves to wondering why I sat there exposing myself to view with my tiny hands and arms. They would see my outstretched, straining hands first thing, and me behind my book looking like a little child conducting a train. As for my father's regular customers, who had to find something to say, they would ask me in a joking tone whether I thought I was at home on the balcony going over my lessons.

He never agreed to let me help him with his work. Stay where you are. . . . Sit, sit! he would say, smiling, as he shifted the chair so it sat firmly on the ground, believing his adjusments were making it easier for me to stay put there. So I sat, draping my hands over my belly as if to give them some rest, thinking that if only I could work, the customers might ignore me. If I were filling the little sacks from the big ones, or placing the weights on the tray of the balance scales, or even cleaning the spaces between the sacks, leaning down, stretching my body over their bulk in order to reach every nook and cranny: as long as I did not go back to my seat, where I composed a still-life image for all eyes to see, they might not notice me. Busy with the tasks of the shop and wearing stained, dusty work clothes, I would seem to be where I belonged. Work, and the clothes for it, and keeping busy not only amidst the sacks of goods for sale but also among the noisy stalls, whose vendors are always shouting out for customers—these were activities suited to malformed bodies. Then it would be like the way it is when you try to hide something under something else that looks very similar. Like using dirt to begrime a face whose skin has already darkened to the color of dust.

There it is. It's there inside the final circle that his pointing finger traces, inside that tight ring he makes, there at the very center, among the other shops he's pointing out; it is inside his final and smallest circle, the smallest possible. He wants us—me and my mother both—to see what his finger points to, because he thinks the only reason he cannot see his shop is his own weak vision. Away, get out of the way! he says to her, peeved. *You*—come here, you. *You* know where it is! he says to me. He begins jerking his finger sideways as if to return himself to the point he lost a few seconds ago. It's there, look, look—you can see it.

I stand close to him, pressed against his arm and hand, but stubbornly I keep my head held rigidly away and my eyes fixed elsewhere, resisting his attempt to drag me, as he does every time, into looking at something I know I will not really be able to see. When he gets annoyed with me for standing there stiff and motionless, refusing to look where he wants me to look, he steps away from me, and then he turns away from my mother and me altogether to face an empty part of the apartment. Even he doesn't know where he wants us to look, she says to me, soothingly. Trying to placate me, she wants to ease me out of the rigid stance that she thinks I must find painful, but which I maintain even after he has stepped away.

He doesn't know where he wants us to look, my mother says. Sometimes she illustrates her words with gestures, sticking out her finger, mimicking his movements, looking far into the distance through narrowed eye slits in imitation of the blind. When she grips my hand as if to dig me out of the predicament into which I have fallen, I know it won't last. I know that she will slip from my grasp the moment we're inside. It's not yet close enough to our next mealtime for her to seat me at the table, both hands guiding me there and holding my chair. But neither will she usher me over to one of the little sofas in the sitting room and sit down across from me — for what would we talk about, sitting there like that? And she doesn't like it when I sit alone reading in the tiny room filled with books, so she certainly won't lead me — my hand gripped tightly in hers — to its door.

He does not know where he wants me to look. He divides the city into circles or sections in order to finally arrive at his shop, which in fact nobody can see unless they're standing immediately in front of it. When they started tearing down the buildings, raising masses of dust and smoke that we could see from our home, he would declare, There's the place, the shop's in there. Just like that, he'd say it, as he pointed his fingers vaguely in several directions.

Yesterday, it was over there, my mother would retort. She gestured in the one direction he was not pointing to, where no dust and smoke rose. Anyway, she observed, it wouldn't take all of this to topple it. All it would need is a bulldozer to ram into it, once from this side and once from the other, she says with one finger on each hand rapping sharply against what she imagines as the shop walls.

As for the nearby vegetable market, which had spilled out across the paved alleyway, they would have only to knock down a single stand for the whole thing to collapse into itself, domino-like, as if the structures were lightweight tents leaning against each other. Dynamite is only for the tall buildings, my mother said to him before she began counting off the names of buildings she knew: The Hijaziyya Building, the Pharaon Building, the Maqasid Building, the . . .

I have retired! he would bark, breaking in to interrupt the stream of names. I have retired, and I'm too old to work, he would say peevishly. Now it was her, he thought. She herself was delivering the blows to his shop, causing it to collapse under the weight of the big names that flattened it, name after name, blow upon blow, hammering it into the ground that soon enough would erase almost all trace of it.

I'm worn out, he would say with finality, bringing the feud to a halt before it could drive her to say, as she did every time, that we were eating up the pennies that were meant to be our last resort, and that surely my father was no better than the other merchants who had moved their shops to new locations.

Or perhaps he wanted to cut the quarrel short before he would have to repeat those curt, tired phrases of his. I have retired . . . I'm worn out . . . I am old now. For I am quite certain that all of them were directed wholly at me, who had never yet worked and who was not worn out. I was twenty-three at the time—the year we moved—and I had not taken a single step toward working at anything. All I knew about *work* was what my father did, moving among his customers and his huge open sacks, and maybe also what the vegetable-stand vendors were doing, as their voices reached our shop. In there, whenever I stood up he would say to me, Sit down, sit! as he fiddled with the chair, repositioning it carefully so that its four legs sat evenly and firmly. He was not even willing for me to make the rounds of the restaurant owners, his customers, to collect the day's accumulated debts. Wait for me here, he would tell me as he tugged on his trousers, pulling them up in preparation for a brisk walk. And so I would have to wait for him, sitting on the chair and laying my hands over my stomach as if to give them some needed rest. He thought my hands and arms would tire even from occupations that did not require their repeated use; after all, with the restaurateurs, all I had to do was to collect these small amounts of money and stuff them into my pocket. You stay right here, he would say. Just wait for me here. I was invariably too sluggish to respond that I really must do something, that what tired me out was all of this sitting on his chair. But I had no familiarity with any kind of work beyond his comings and goings and those of the vendors close by. In the shop, after a customer walked out onto the street, purchases in hand, he would talk to me as a father ought to talk to his son about his future. You should be a watchmaker, he would say. That's the sort of thing that would suit you well. He was thinking that my extraordinarily small hands would be comfortable working with such small objects, and deft with them, too. Merely saying it gave him some comfort, since it meant my future would be a natural and ordinary one. My work might even be an improvement on his, something better than the labor of the man who was my father. You were made for that, he would say to me, imagining me sitting at a table covered with tiny instruments, a watch between my hands that was so small I seemed to repair it by simply by training my eyes on it. That's where you belong, down there, he would say to me as he pointed toward the watchmakers' shops, which were not very far from ours. Those unsoiled shops whose proprietors, inside them, were also clean and neat and orderly, just as I was whenever I left the house, wearing the clothes that my mother had washed and ironed.

I have retired . . . I am worn out, he would announce to my mother, and I would think that what was tiring him out was the tedium of sitting at home. No more than three or four months had passed since he had lapsed into this state of inactivity. Back then his body had held so much excess energy that he'd had to channel it toward me, for needs I did not have. Stand up! he would say. Get up off the chair so we can make certain it's sitting evenly. Or: Are you hungry? He would ask me the question just so he could go out and come back with something for me to eat. Or I would hear: Shall I buy you a magazine to read? Sitting at home irritated and wearied him. Or perhaps the weariness really was a result of all the hours he had spent in the shop, and as it accumulated he had kept it hidden inside, waiting to show itself. You—sit down, now. Sit down. And so I sat. I would not rise from that chair except to ask him if he needed my help or to simply make as if to ask him. Sit down, sit down there! and so I would sit down, to put him at rest. It contented him to feel that he was handling his work and taking care of me, all at the same time.

II

ONLY OUR BUILDING BROKE UP the sandy expanse that stretched beyond it, rippling out in tiny waves that looked like a landscape of miniature hills. And beyond the sand there was nothing; if we were to walk all the way to the end of it, it seemed, we would find that same kind of downward slope that we see from our balcony, separating us from the old city. Only our building interrupted the sandy way that continued on behind it in an accumulation of drifts. Solitary, it rose up in that emptiness like a squat tower. From where I was sitting, in the little room where I have my books, I could hear the sound of a spoon clattering to the floor on the level below us. Hearing every tinny reverberation it made, I guessed that nothing was happening in the building at that particular moment other than that spoon falling. Through the open window I could hear the movements of the man and the woman on the ground floor as they tended the plants just outside; I heard their every move so exactly that it was as if I was seeing them with my eyes.

Through the window, too, I can rest my eyes—as my father had put it—by looking out at the sand and the stalks the sand yields, before it proceeds to dry them out and then finally to burn them. When we moved to this home of ours

21

thirteen years ago, my father worked this particular window over and over, gripping the handle and opening and closing it repeatedly as if trying to ease its stiffness for my hands. He also wanted to make me understand that I would have to open and shut it like that to bring in the clean outside air—the sort of fresh air that had never reached as far as my cramped room in the old place. That room hadn't been anything more than a short narrow hallway lined by three doors, one of which opened onto the toilet whose odor my mother was always worrying would poison me. The more cramped she saw the hallway becoming as I added more books to its shelves, the more insistently she would ask me why I didn't move, along with my belongings, to the spacious room that remained empty. We won't ask you for the rent, she would say to me teasingly, before adding in an affectionate tone that the room was mine; she and my father would not be having another child.

You have a window here, my father said to me as he poked his head out to smell the pure outside air. He was delighted with that window on the day we moved in. Our first day here. Standing in the doorway to my room, about to leave, he shifted his gaze back and forth between that window and me; it seemed as if he wanted to reassure himself that the two of us—the window and I—would stay together here, remaining close neighbors, even clinging to each other. He figured that I would spend all of my time in the room, since we had no shop for me to go to, and no particular route to walk. He assumed the same about my mother and himself. As he shut the door to my room, it seemed to me that he was shutting the door to each room on the scene that ought to unfold within it, and closing the door would preserve the tableau. My mother, for instance, would have to be in the kitchen for him to close its door so contentedly. Likewise, she must be in the dining room for him to see it looking exactly as he wanted it, perfect and complete. In those first days of transition, freshly moved into our new home, we had to take on our final and definitive image, as if nothing in our life was henceforth to change. Closing the door on me, he saw what he was doing now as one of his very final gestures, to be completed by his closing the other doors and, afterwards, sitting in repose on the balcony and beginning the long, slow interval that was his life now.

I would be in the room behind its closed door as my father and mother sat down, separately, to survey this home's order, each from their own point of view. Or they would be roaming through it, she wanting to satisfy herself that all was arranged correctly and he reassuring himself that everything was in its proper place. Or they would stand together in the kitchen, agreeing or differing on what my mother was preparing or cooking.

In the days that followed our move she reminded him repeatedly that we would be returning to the city we had vacated when *they* finished the work they were doing there. With his lack of employment, she saw him becoming like those house husbands who spend their time observing and commenting on their wives' every act. Tomorrow, soon, we're going back, she would say to him, as if to divert him from his preoccupation with her food preparation. He wouldn't answer, and indeed he appeared to have heard nothing at all, since he simply went on staring at whatever her knife was chopping, poised and waiting for the moment when he would whip his finger toward whatever it was he did not approve of.

He would only pull himself away if he saw me entering the kitchen. He would open the refrigerator door as soon as he thought I was heading for it, and turn toward me, asking if I wanted water. Accompanying me to the door of my room, carrying the water bottle to spare me the task, he seemed no longer able to imagine me in any guise but that which I offered as I stood before him. He could no longer envision me anywhere else; he could not locate a place for me in which I would look any different than I did here before him. Ever since we had vacated our shop, he no longer knew how or where to position me in a future that would be mine. The watchmakers who had worked not far from us, and who he had thought would easily take me in, had gone away just as we had done, leaving behind their sturdy shops, fortified little spaces like empty vaults. He no longer knew where people went about doing whatever it was they meant to do. He stopped saying to me that the most suitable employment I could have would be watch-making, and that he would be happy—thrilled, even—to imagine me sitting at a table littered with tiny precision tools and parts. When he began making those rounds of his—which in any case soon began to leave him irritated—he was earnestly trying to keep himself entertained by observing his old acquaintances in their new circumstances. Houri is making the sandwiches for his customers himself now, he would exclaim to my mother, laughing as if at some private joke as he recalled the man wrapping bread around the sandwich filling. Or he would tell her that now Kilani was selling chirpy little birds and multicolored fish meant to liven up people's sitting rooms. Better than him sitting at home, my mother retorted, knowing perfectly well that her words would accomplish one thing: they would immediately silence him, and then, a moment later, he would escape to the balcony where he could be alone, gazing down to the point where the building met the sand.

When he began saying to her that he had gotten tired, that he had retired and grown old, he was blocking his own path to gradually returning, finding himself renting a new shop and buying new goods to stock it with. I am here, he would say to her, his palms flat and arms outstretched to encompass an open space, as if describing the borders of our home as the place where inevitably he would always, ever and only be. I am *here*, he would say, as a peremptory summing up (for her benefit) of his already concise, staccato sentence that he was *tired retired and old*. Then he would draw himself away from wherever they were standing or sitting together, staying in the apartment but putting between them a space he thought was ample enough to restore the state of silent feud between them.

He would go with me as far as the door to my room, where he would hand me the water bottle. After all, he had lifted it from my grasp not only to spare me the fatigue, but also to perform one of the functions that he thought demonstrated the importance of his presence in this house. Standing next to my mother and observing every chop of her knife was another one of those functions he fulfilled, as was making the rounds of the sitting room, between the small sofas, peering at them and at what was around them as he headed for the front entryway, to inspect it and to check the main door. His role was here: in the house, *inside* the house that he would continually monitor, taking care of it over and above my mother's care for its cleanliness and arrangement. And in charge of its proper running, which meant he was permanently prepared for prompt action if the knife blade were to nick my mother's hand. What this meant was that, from the second she said to him that the knife was making her hand shake, he would bark out, Right, yes, I'm coming, as though he were responding to an anticipated incident whose eventuality he had been clocking, moment by moment.

He was here, truly at home, where he wanted me—like him—to be. Inside. He no longer said to me that working as a watchmaker would suit me very well. The way he saw it, my being here, in the house, *inside*, was better for me. It would make me better, more relaxed, more comfortable. And anyway, the watchmakers had not gone back to work: in his rounds, he had not seen a single watchmaker's shop. So that we would believe him—my mother and I—he would add that perhaps they did have shops but he had certainly not seen any of them. Then he would observe that the streets where all of these buildings were going up were so many that a body could hardly believe that the people who packed them now had actually all fit into the old city. My mother knew very well that these statements of his were of a piece with his declarations that he would not ever return to work. So she would respond that the old city had fallen into ruin because there were so many people and its streets were not spacious enough to hold them. He wouldn't answer; perhaps he didn't even hear her, or perhaps he heard but paid no attention to the sense of her words because he was so fixed on her face and its expressions as she spoke. No, he no longer spoke of my perfect future as a watchmaker. Ever since the watchmakers had vacated their shops, he had begun to find it too hard to imagine me sitting and working, or standing in the doorway of the shop where I worked, looking out at a landscape that he would not know.

When he had said to me that working as a watchmaker would suit me perfectly, it had required only a little imagination. Just like that, he could shove aside one of those watchmakers whom he knew and seat me in his place, at his very table. It would be simple enough for us, he thought, to arrive at our respective workplaces, walking together, with the same distance to cover, the same length of a walk that had long been habitual, ever since those days when we left the house together to go to his shop. We would have to arrive at my shop first, though, not his, so that he could unlock the place and go with me as far as the door where he would say goodbye, exactly as he does here every time he hands me the water bottle that he has carried for me before shutting the door and returning alone to the kitchen.

He is here, at home. He gets up in the morning exactly as he did when he went to work, hurrying to begin his activities right away. He looks at my mother first, as he stands still for a moment next to his bed to reassure himself that she is still there asleep on her bed. Then he walks to my room to find out, from behind the firmly shut door, whether I have awoken yet or I'm still sleeping. Then to the front doorway to see if it is still locked as he shut and locked it yesterday. Then to the pair of windows over there, opening their wooden shutters to give the house daylight. Then to the kitchen, running his eyes across it, like so, as if he forgot what condition he had left it in yesterday before going to bed. Then to the big balcony to cast his eyes, which will not do anything for him, over the old city. From the minute he wakes up, he begins this work of his, so aptly named by my mother *household guard duty*. From the inside, not from the outside, she says, in contrast to the government's night sentries. She calls it the same thing when he stands next to her in the kitchen staring at what her hands are cleaning or chopping before she puts it in its pot or container. Look, he's decided it is time we sleep, she says to me when he gets up from where we're sitting on the balcony to go in and close windows and doors. Hey, it's the wee hours already, she says to me. She may be joking but she means that my father does not just keep watch over the house but sets its hours too.

And he triumphs. Once he begins shutting the doors and windows, it isn't long before my mother begins to yawn. We have gotten sleepy, she says, regaining her breath, which her yawning had momentarily overwhelmed. She stands up, but before heading for bed she spends an entire minute looking at us without saying a word, to gauge what we will look like, out here, as she falls asleep on her pillow.

Tonight, sleep in your bedroom, she says to me, noticing me getting to my feet just as she has done. I have some pages to read, I respond immediately, getting my words in before my father makes the very same request, but in the form of a question: Why don't you sleep in your bedroom tonight? That's exactly how he speaks to me, as he closes the heavy double doors, one over the other, careful to keep them from making anything more than the very faintest sound of metal on metal. It makes nothing stronger than a light *takka* followed by the sound of the bolt, a light sound too, but one that emphatically closes and locks our entire home.

III

I GET TO MY FEET, not to go and finish reading those remaining pages of my book but so that my father can conclude the closing-up chores with which he winds up the day. From my window the sand, made lustrous by the moonlight, looks silvery and close, as if its surface has risen toward me. The moonlight seems to carry the sand almost right to me. Or perhaps that light is simply strengthening my vision as I look at the sand, shining so brilliantly and so brazenly that soon it repels my gaze. Sitting on the balcony, we can catch the sound of the breeze as it approaches, winding up to us from below—that faraway below where the old city lies. The moonlight gives us the city, too, but as nothing more than skeletal outlines of buildings, ash-gray with age and remoteness. We send our gazes there, to perch at the margins of its ring-shaped expanse, to know that something of us remains there.

I will complete the evening's togetherness alone, sitting at the window. Opening that window, I seemed to be breaching the wall of our home or displaying its interior spaces to the outside world from which it has sealed itself off. But there is nothing out there but the glistening sand below me, which lies still and silent as if the light falling on it freezes it in

29

place, fixing its image forever. I am waiting, though. I am expecting a light to come on in the room below. It's the room exactly below mine—below me—on the floor directly beneath, and it will not be for more than a moment or two, that soft yellow light peculiar to homes, as it escapes the room and plunges across a stretch of sand. The instant I see it, I am up from my chair and at the window frame, doubling my body over the sill to dangle my head below. But all I can see is a row or two of tiles, bare and empty as if the people down there have removed all traces of furniture, shifting them to the room's far end.

Still, I can see her in my mind. I imagine her picking up whatever it was she came in to get and then (with her other hand, the one that's not occupied) pressing the light switch to *off*. Her small hand is stained with ink in the way of schoolgirls, and the skin around her fingernails is crusty and flaky. It's only an instant or two, and when the moment ends I am still hanging out over the windowsill, pressing my stomach against it as I stretch downward as far as I can go. As long as no one can see me, I am in no hurry to bring my feet back to meet the floor. Anyway, she might come back. She might come back to get something else she needs: a colored ribbon, a belt to encircle her waist, or something else of the sort.

And I know, too, that their evening together—theirs, too—is over. I know this from the shadow that comes to meet the expanse of light and then advances fully halfway across the area of sand lit up by the light in her room. I know it also from the pair of plump hands that reach for the wooden shutters to close them. She will be in bed and already well on her way to falling asleep when the voice of the woman—her mother's voice—says a couple of words to hasten her sleep, and then when the woman's fleshy hand turns out the light. I will not wait long before letting the light in my room run out over the sand. But my light will make only stripes, piercing the slatted wood of the shutters, which are already closed.

I do not sit down to read the remaining pages of the book I have left open on the table. There is no activity that truly suits this time of evening. In the course of the day, I did not tire out my body so that it would demand the onset of night and claim the respite of sleep. And it's also true that books we want to read in daylight contain occurrences and episodes and fierce words that don't suit dwelling upon at night. There is nothing quite right for this time of night, and I can find nothing to do other than reading some passages in that book or lying down and waiting to drop off to sleep. Or I can do both at once by planting the book next to me in bed and leaving the light on. I can do both at once, reading and sleeping, since I have prepared myself as much for one as for the other, and because I keep them both right here beside me. I protect myself with my book, or perhaps I'm losing myself in it to keep away the loneliness into which my sleeplessness may well plunge me. But I do start off trying to conquer my wakefulness, closing my eyes to test how complete it is, finding it absolute. When I give up and open my eyes, I know without a doubt that I have been ousted from the house of sleep and I will have to get there by means of some ruse. I'll have to get there by a back way or a side street and definitely not by going in through the front door. No, I did not wear out my body during the day that it might fall asleep on its own. I did not use it for anything or expose it to anything. After all, my father closed the doors and all of the windows with his own hands as if he wanted us to go to sleep like guests pampered by the finest service. By day he walks me from the kitchen to the door of my room, keeping watch over me and relieving me of even having to carry a bottle of water. Sit down, sit! he says to me, pulling the chair back from the dining room table so that I can sit down. Once I am seated he tells me to lift myself up slightly so that he can push the chair closer, for the sake (as he sees it) of bringing my hands near enough to reach the table.

When I doze off unexpectedly I'm awake again almost immediately, and it's not a question of real sleep, for these sudden naps leave me feeling more alert than ever. They arrive like a temporary inner disturbance that throws the body off balance for a minute or two. That is not sleep. It is not even the beginnings of sleep, since my wakefulness—even if it takes its time—returns stronger and more aggressive than ever. I have to start fighting it, going back to the very beginning, waiting patiently for another wave of drowsiness that might possibly be real this time and might set me on the path to sleep. But when this one comes it is just as shallow and quick to pass as the others. I know it is, because I can tell that the soft-edged images floating and bobbing through my head have ceased. I do my best to get them back before they can fade out completely, and then I wait, hoping the colors I've regained will bring forth another and longer round of fluid, evanescent images.

Retrieving those images, fixing them in my mind, means I can at least claim a little territory gained in my battle for victory over my sleeplessness. I did not tire my body out today. I didn't tire out even a single body part. Not my trunk, not my limbs. I did nothing that would encourage sleep to inhabit a worn-out toe or finger, foot or hand, and then to gradually occupy the rest of my body. Nightfall makes no difference: when evening comes this body is exactly as it was in the morning. A single unchanging level of energy runs through it no matter what the time of day or night, as evenly distributed across all its parts as it is across the moments I live. A body wrapped in its singular unvarying energy, lying here in the middle of the bed, beneath the light coming from the fixture overhead. The light turns me into something almost like an invalid laid out full length beneath it, still and passive as if I'm waiting for something to be done to me—this strong light from the overhead lamp that I must turn off. I must get up and go over to the switch and flick it off. It is no longer shielding me from this wakefulness that I myself induced and stoked from the moment I began to overcome it. I have to get up and go over to the switch, even though by doing so I know I am being foolish, for I'm taking a chance that this wakefulness will seize me again, and I'm also stupidly risking the possibility that in the heavy darkness my struggle will only intensify. But I have to turn out the light. Then I collapse hurriedly into bed so that I won't be up and about for long.

Colliding waves follow close upon one another through my body. The wave swells and crests, and I know that inside it the pair of fighting beasts has managed to get across the bit of space that was keeping them apart. Here they are now, bodies interlocked in a ceaseless bellowing rage. They have fallen upon each other and entangled themselves; I can see them very clearly. Their thick furry hides are in plain sight, still clean in this moment before the claws bloody them. They are here in front of me even if there is no space for them to stand. Simply two beasts: alone, nothing with them, nothing surrounding them. And as the wave begins to recede, while it is still cresting, I know that I have fallen into some sort of sleep, or I have gone missing, but I know just as well that the wakefulness has vanquished me anyway.

IV

THE OLD MIRROR THEY LUGGED here for me from our old home: why didn't they hang it some other way, not like this, so very high up? In that room housing my bed and wardrobe, I had to step back from the mirror—back and farther back, just to see my face. Not for very long, since all I needed to do while standing at that distance was to trace the part in my hair with my comb and go over it more firmly, pulling the hair away from the comb's path and smoothing it above and below. I still comb it this way, parting it from the roots as I first learned to do, or perhaps as I grew accustomed to doing, since I don't remember my hair looking any other way than this, with a part. In my room here in our new home, where I both read and sleep, I can peer into the mirror from a normal distance, but only if I stand on the bed and hoist myself up to match its height. My part is still there, just as it has always been, marching the same route, but the closer I bring my head to the mirror, the more desiccated it looks: the skin is so dry that it's flaking. The hairs around that part have grown coarse, their ends crinkling and frizzing so that from another angle of my head they give the appearance of a thick raised pad.

Nothing about my appearance has changed. Growing a

moustache has not helped me to look my age, since very little moustache hair actually appeared, and the color, which was already light, has bleached with exposure. So my moustache does not stand out from my face and adds nothing to it. No, nothing in my face has changed—not only in the time since its reflection in this same mirror when it last hung in our old home, but also from an earlier time, when I was thirteen years old, which was when I began to stare into it as if I had to accustom myself to my own image. I perceived somehow that this was my final image and I would never have another one. Or perhaps the crucial moment is when I began at that same age of thirteen to imagine how my face appeared to the eyes of whoever looked at me, and to feel, when they did look at me, that I was seeing myself exactly as they were seeing me.

I see the image of my face alone in that mirror placed so high, floating there without my body beneath it. If I want to see that, it won't be in the mirror but rather with a gaze downward. I have liked sensing my face and my body being looked at separately, as detached parts of me, because that means my face is seen as it is, by and for itself. Indeed, at that age of thirteen I could almost believe that people saw me as I wished to be seen; I could convince myself that they—like me—overlooked whatever they did not like to see in me. But in outsize mirrors, the kind we sit across from in barber shops or find ourselves suddenly, unexpectedly facing in the window glass of clothing stores and cinemas, I can't help but see how my body, puffed out in front, all but assaults my face simply by reaching all the way up to it. In the bus's rectangular mirror, into which I kept stealing continuous but furtive glances all day long throughout that school trip, I had to notice how the puffiness began at my lower belly and rose to swell across my chest, forcing my head to sit awkwardly above it. Trying to minimize this puffed-up appearance of mine, I worked to raise my body upward, sitting as if I were standing, but only from the midsection up. It tired me out. Sitting there, on the front seat in the bus near the mirror, I knew I was exposing myself to their stares—or to her stare, among the rest of them. But, I thought, the noisy commotion they made would stay in the back and would keep them there, on the bus's long back seat and in the empty space in front of it. Staying close to the mirror, I could maintain my watch over what was going on behind me. I could keep it all under my gaze, remaining attentive and careful not to be caught unaware by letting go or dozing off, which would expose me even more.

I also thought that by sitting there—and staying near the mirror—I could keep her under my gaze. It was not long, though, before the partygoers singing in the back of the bus attracted her. When she left her seat and wandered back toward them, they began beating the *tabla* more loudly, the drumbeat celebrating her capture. That's what they did whenever anyone left their seat to join them. I could see her in the mirror in front of me, standing still with some space separating her from them, as though it were enough to watch them from a distance and enjoy the din they were creating. When she leaned against one of the seats, her back to the mirror, I suddenly thought they would beat the drum louder especially for her, inviting her now to sit on the broad seat they occupied or to stand among their fans in the open space in front of it. But she didn't; rather, from time to time she twisted around to look behind her, at the first three rows of seats where no one remained seated but me. No, there was no one there but me, looking into the mirror, stealing furtive glances at her. It was as though, when she looked toward where I sat, she was trying to make certain that I was still there, sitting and waiting, staying exactly where I had been a moment before.

Or as if, when she turns to look in my direction, she is trying to make me understand that she apologizes for keeping her distance, or that she is just marking some time, waiting so that when she comes over to me it will look natural, like a mere coincidence as everyone redistributes themselves in the bus once the band in back has grown quiet as they take a break. Or she will make it appear as if coming here is just a matter of falling into the seat next to me as the bus shudders or swerves. Or she will seem to be coming deliberately, making it seem as though she has come especially to say a few words that have just come into her mind and that she wants very much to say to someone whose presence, also, has just come into her mind. Or she will come and sit with me, keeping me company, on the pretext—which she will not actually have to explain to anyone—that I am sitting by myself and someone really ought to talk to me.

But the place I had left empty beside me since climbing onto the bus remained empty. They did reoccupy other seats, redistributing themselves several times as they rested after singing a set or returning to the bus after little excursions outside. But the seat next to me remained empty. Alone, I stayed in my seat, leaving the proper amount of space clear so that someone could come and sit down if they wanted to do so. Their games would bring them to particular seats that they would soon vacate, only to land on other seats also for a very short time. But I went on sitting in my seat in that place that had become mine. Even though I left the bus twice (just as they did) to take a short walk, I watched myself return to the very same seat, plastering myself to the wall of the bus and the window and leaving the place next to me empty.

It was up to me to get up and go over to them, where they sat at the back of the bus, and to make myself part of their noisy fun. Probably it would have been better for me that way, because I could have made them forget my body, not by keeping it distant and hunched over itself but rather by losing it—by making it disappear among the movements and gestures I would extort from it. If I were to clap, that is what they would notice, not my pair of tiny hands and the way one flops against the other. If I were to attempt dancing with them they would see my flexing body simply as a series of moves, as if the maneuvers I made were a cloud of dust I would raise to distract their gaze away from me and to occupy her with something other than what she ought not see. I should have been there among them at the back of the bus. But while it was happening, while I was on that school trip, I did not see this until it was already too late. The time in which I could have changed something had already passed. She had stopped looking in that particular direction, that section of the bus where I sat. In fact, I couldn't help but notice—in the mirror—how her attention was now turning entirely to them; how, the more she laughed at what they were doing, the more fully she appeared to have forgotten that only a few moments earlier she had been turning to gaze at me. She forgot, or else she was distracted from looking at me by something else that was going on.

Every time they climbed down from the bus for a little excursion, leaving their *tabla* behind on the back seat that stretched the width of the bus, I felt as I stared at them— through the windowpane this time, not in the front mirror— that their only reason for mounting all of that noisy fun was to demonstrate how adept they were at suddenly stopping the clamor and quieting down. Their close huddle would break apart as they moved away from the bus. Four of them grouped together, five, and then three; and there was the last quartet who waited at the door of the bus until their number was complete. Coming back to the bus they would be more scattered and chaotic, looking as though they were rushing to reach it, afraid it might leave without them.

But, returning to the bus, they will leave behind a couple of walkers dawdling along or trailing their caravan. Through the window I can see one of them walking as slowly as possible next to the girl who accompanies him. And then there's the one who will come into view as he turns onto the street— for I can see all the way to the head of this street: she will be beside him, walking slowly and lowering her head to study a bit of fauna or a flower she'll twirl between her palms. I knew it would be her, coming into sight next to him, because she was not among the first group to arrive back at the bus. She is just visible now at the corner, walking at a leisurely pace until she reaches the two steps into the bus. She climbs them slowly, still in no hurry. When we are all on the bus and it moves off, she is not where she was before, inside their little circle, for she has chosen a seat somewhere in the middle, to be alone with him and away from them, and also to keep herself apart from where I sit, another girl altogether now, as if, when she first climbed onto the bus, she did not even hint to me that she had been eagerly awaiting this outing of ours, this trip we would make together.

V

FROM THE WINDOW IN THE room overlooking the sand track (the room my father calls mine, the room he entreats me to sleep in, night after night) I can see the girl who lives just below me as she steps out of the building's front entrance. I will already be in wait, there behind the window where I have been busying myself with a towel, drying my face, neck, and hands. It won't be more than a few moments before she appears, hoisting her bulky book bag and walking heavily. She drags herself along as if she hasn't yet rid herself of the sleep from which she was suddenly and unwillingly yanked. As her feet take their first steps, her body swerves toward the edge of the track: final traces of sleep still hold her in their sway. I know very well that I really should not be standing at the window so expectantly. If I stand here like this every day, I am behaving exactly like those people who are too obviously expecting something, or (even worse) I am one of those who lie in wait, anticipating a response to the look they send out. No, I must not stand like this, waiting behind the window. Girls her age activate something in those who watch them, but it's wrong. It's errant desire, misplaced desire. It's something defective in the men who watch.

I watch her slowing down, maybe stumbling, and I figure

that she must be taking in the fact that between her and the end of the sand track there is still a long and arduous way to go. Her feet sink into the sand, and I worry about sharp grains of it finding their way into her soft white shoes and soiling her socks, which are also white. But every day at this time, I know, she will stamp her feet on the cement surface where the sand track ends abruptly. She wants to knock away the sandy soil that clings and at the same time announce to herself that she has finished with the track that so annoys her. She stamps her feet twice, then a third time to finally rid the white shoes of the sand and its dirty, clinging residue. But the sand that has worked its way inside will stay there, sticking to her socks, suspended between her soft and pliable toes, which are not yet roughened or cracked by age or by too much walking.

When she reaches the closest edge of the building where she will wait for the bus, I can no longer see her from my window. Once she is there, I turn away from the window and hurriedly finish rubbing my face and neck dry, as if to proclaim to myself that it is time for things to move on to the next stage. Come to the table! says my father as he stands gazing at the plates, which aren't very many and anyway, aren't full. He lets me have the few minutes I need to go into my room and get into my daytime clothes. Come to the table! he says to my mother, this time going to her in the kitchen. Or he might just stand at the door waiting for her, just inside the central hallway where he can also see me leaving the room that holds all the books. He waits to see which one of us will come out first, me or my mother. Come on, let's eat, he says to me as he takes a couple of steps toward me as if to meet me so that we can proceed together, as companions, to our places in the dining room.

There are not many dishes on the table. And they're

the same ones we saw at breakfast, the same ones that are set down on the table every day. They are dishes whose contents never vary. We try to make up for it, though, by sitting down together and then, when we finish eating, by carrying the plates together into the kitchen. Back in our old home, my mother cooked something new every day even though we could have eaten perfectly well from leftovers of the day before. Trying to tell her not to tire herself out, when my father returned home from his shop he would declare that she was cooking food on top of food! At breakfast we would slice thin slivers of cheese from the large rounds that my father so carefully and elaborately selected—naming each kind—from the grocers near his shop.

Come to the table! my father calls with a vigor that suggests he is summoning us to an overflowing banquet, or at least to a seating that will last longer than the five or ten minutes we will actually sit there, rising quickly afterward to carry the few plates into the kitchen. My mother intones her proverb to remind us how anxious she is: We eat our own flesh if no pennies come afresh! But she no longer has it in her heart to demand that my father must search for a new shop, nor that we must economize more. For she has left to my father the business of figuring out the balance between available funds and time remaining, which of course no one can predict. She's scolding us again, says my father, exasperated but unable to let it go. How?! he asks. How can a woman who does not know how to add two numbers together have in her head the sum of money we spend daily against the amount of money we have left?

But even while saying this, my mother did not truly mean that my father should go on looking for a new shop. And no one was saying that I would need to find work either.

The watchmakers had scattered after leaving their old work-shops. It was no longer possible for my father to imagine me sitting in one of those dark shops, bringing a watch up to my eyes, perched on a chair behind a table in a place he would know well, where the surroundings would be so utterly fa-miliar. In fact, now, none of us could really imagine any real change to our situation, now that we were so accustomed to ordering our life around the few matters we could still arrange in our reduced circumstances: a spare amount of food and as part of that ration, a portion of meat that was far too minimal. Cut it into smaller pieces! my father demands of my mother, leaning forward to peer even more closely at the knife she wields, his pointing finger accusing the meat. It's the right thing to do, he feels, since after all, the dam-age meat causes is greater than the benefit it brings. Cut it smaller, he tells her, meaning the meat, and then he will tell her, as she is beginning to cook it, that the fat causes more harm than good. These little things that we find our-selves doing every day as if they are necessary, like getting up to go off to bed the moment my father starts closing and locking windows and doors, like living and moving about in the apartment exactly as we have always done. My mother restores order to the modest chaos we cause by sitting on the balcony. She returns the cushions to their official positions, as if by doing so she can bring the chairs back to a pristine state untouched by our use.

By the same token, he no longer asks me if I would like him to buy me a magazine to read. As for the books—well, I have a lot of them already, he thinks. Ever since our move, the question he has directed at me will take on another mean-ing in his eyes whenever he looks at the books: Will you really be able to read all of them? He believes the time has come for these books I bought but still have not read, even now. I have a lot of them, he thinks, and as he watches me heading into the room after breakfast, he believes I will spend valuable time in there, with those books of mine, and yet it will not cost us anything. There's no doubt in my mind, in fact, that he thinks books are more lasting than other objects. After all, they're amenable to storage and preservation. Aging does not detract from their worth.

After breakfast each of us withdraws into our own work. My mother hoists a mass of greens into the sink. My father stands just behind or next to her as if on guard duty. They seem to find it reassuring that I'm sitting in the room reading. When the two of them, or even just one of them, walks down the hallway that runs up to its door, they are wary of the sound their feet make, lest it annoy me or distract me from my reading. They act as if I am the only one in this house whose activities should oblige others to limit the noise they make, weighing every movement and every word according to my needs. As they see it, I am the one who is working. Or I am the one who is preparing himself for work, as though I'm a student finally on the verge of mastering his chosen specialization. My father lifts his index finger to his lips, sealing them although they are already closed, so that my mother will realize that whatever she is doing is producing loud sounds. When he crosses over to the hallway I can all but see him lift his foot fully off the floor so that he can put it down slowly and precisely, as if to detach its transit from the movement of his other foot, which he will raise just like the first one but not until the first one is firmly on the floor. He believes it is possible to derive some hope from all of this time that I spend sitting and reading. It must amount to something, even if he does not know what it is, or what signs to look for that will announce this *something* when it does actually begin.

You read as much in one day as students read in a month! he exclaims when he sees me finally emerge from the room. This is his way of encouraging me and making me feel I'm almost at the finish line, and that when I'm there I'll be the winner. This does not please my mother, though. She still believes that my frail body will not be strong enough in the end to endure all of this reading. You're making him ill! she snaps at my father, who—with a dismissive wave of his hand—quiets her before he swings his whole body and face in my direction. He is ready for action. He asks me whether there is anything I would like him to do for me.

VI

AMONG THOSE SINGING AND DANCING on the bus, that young fellow who went off alone with her on the walk, returning at the last possible minute, monopolized her not only during the excursion but later on, too. In the long file of students winding from the recreation area to the classrooms, I saw her standing in front of the door to her classroom, waiting, and I could see the look she gave him even though there were seven or eight students between us. It was a look that did not dissolve quickly; she concluded it slowly by lowering her eyelids. She closed her eyes as though she had been met with resistance or aversion and was determined to respond, but not too quickly, by showing the same reaction. There, at the door to her classroom, she kept her eyes closed for about as long as it took for two or three students to shuffle by. When she opened them again, she seemed—in her silence—to have traveled miles away from the normal pursuits of students. She had disengaged from the others, or perhaps she had suddenly matured, and it was as if she had introduced into the school a whiff of what happens between adults, outside.

This look that, giving it, then impeded her and impelled her to respond with like resistance. . . . In the time that separated the excursion's end from her standing like this at her classroom door, many things must have happened between them, since they did not appear—judging from that exchanged look—to be simply completing what they had begun during the jaunt. They had already completed it, surely, in that short time, and then had stepped back, abandoning it, or one of them had, and then they resumed it, to carry it to completion once again. Many things had happened between them. And she—having closed her eyes for the time it took for two or three students to walk by—did not care what she might make plain in front of the students. And then she, when she opened her eyes, did not really see the students who passed by after him, one by one in file. She did not see me. I knew that before I drew even with her, yet still I hurried on so that I could quickly disappear. Even if her mind were elsewhere, engrossed in thoughts of him, I did not want to parade by her, walking in that queue in which I stood out, having to hop and scurry, thrusting my chest upward like one of those shore birds that hop on their little feet, since the smallness of their wings keeps them from flying.

When I said to my father that I would not go back to school, he thought immediately that the students had gone back to teasing and upsetting me by imitating my walk and the way I moved my hands. Indeed he seemed completely confident in his suspicions, which were based on things I used to say when I was a small boy. Tomorrow, I would declare, I am not going back to school. And then I would go quiet, waiting for him to ask me which children had harassed me. This time, though, he had to keep himself from being overly hasty, because it did occur to him that boys of this age had other ways to trouble and upset someone like me. You won't go back to school? he asked me, as if to give himself more time to comprehend, on his own, what they might be

48

doing to me. While I waited for him, silent, I knew that he would begin his guessing from the very same starting point. Does it tire you out to carry your schoolbag when you walk to school? Does it bother you to sit so long in class? When you're sitting there does something start hurting?

So let him leave school, said my mother: I can still see her saying it. Let him stop going, she said as she poked her needles into the wool and added a stitch to the rose-pink pullover she was making for herself. School tires him out, she added without lifting her eyes from the row she was working. Before she could add anything more in that way she has of appearing not to really care, or not to be paying attention, my father told her she did not know what school means because she had never studied at one.

What will you do instead? he asked me after satisfying himself that he had squelched her interference in matters she did not understand. Will you work or will you sit at home?

He spoke to me without implying in the slightest that someone like me can only work at the kind of tasks that are taught in school. That eased my mind, because it meant he was offering me a broader range of things I might do rather than suddenly restricting my choices with his words. But his irritation surfaced as soon as my mother remarked that I could study at home. A look of anger on his face, he wheeled round to face her squarely, to make her comprehend—to warn her, even—that she must stop talking about things she simply did not understand. Now I could sense his exasperation, even though when he turned to me, he merely asked me the same question he had posed a moment before. Will you work or will you sit at home?

In his fury he looked as though he wanted to hear a single answer with a single meaning. As though he wanted me to answer, for example, that I would work, but only so that he could then come back with a second question to which, also, he wanted a single and anticipated answer. And what work will you do? His face maintained an expression that was both insistent and closed. Will you work or will you sit in the house? he asked me a third time, as if to get me to understand that he would not let up until he heard that single clear answer, with no hesitation, and no stumbling over my words.

She made him so angry. He did not ask me what had annoyed me at school, since he didn't want to appear to be taking my side. This is what happened every time I said I would not return to school. She really did know how to upset him. He began staring into my face as if he could elicit my answer more quickly. The longer I took over it, the more I amplified his rage and his fury. His facility at giving little compliments to his customers and the breezy good humor he practiced in front of them did nothing to attenuate this force of his. It was a force only his anger could awaken. His fury manifested when he disagreed with someone else, but it always seemed more like he was fighting with himself. You want to sit in the house? he asked me, but this time not so he could await my response: rather, he said it to make me understand that if such an idea even came into my head, that meant I was only interested in becoming like women who sit alone all day in empty homes.

But he would come back from wherever it was his anger had taken him as soon as my mother made one of her gestures signaling that her patience was at an end. Getting up from her chair with a muttered insult flung in my father's direction, she went into another room. I pondered her fancy appearance, which I found laughable in the circumstances. Her careful chignon and her dress smocked like a child's gown looked incongruous against her irritable mood, as though in this finery of hers she had been preening herself quietly for some secret but anticipated occasion but had been disappointed when something unexpected and contrary to her plans occurred. At least she put a stop to my father's anger, for even as, in response to her insults, he shouted at her to get out, he noticed that I was at the end of my rope. He knew he'd been harsh to me in a way I could not endure, and now he was sympathy itself to me. Me, for whom such words falling onto my body—which had no defenses, as he saw it—were like so many hard slaps.

From the kitchen where she had gone came the sharp and sullen thuds of pans moving around. I knew she was not planning to use them but merely banging them here and there to show that whatever insults she might be uttering or thinking, she was struggling to keep them confined to the kitchen. And my father did not need much time to come out of his anger. Returning to me, showing he was with me and always at my side, he asked me what had gone on at school. When he was in one of those calm states that always followed his bouts of anger, my father could concede to what he would not have accepted ordinarily, to the point where (apologetically and agreeably) he would position me—and himself along with me—to face precisely whatever it was that a few moments before had sparked his anger.

Now, what will you do if you leave school? But this time he said it as if it were a real question. He said it as if he were saying to me, Come, let's think together what would happen if we were to abandon school. This was the payment I would get for his anger. This was my reward, which, in this peacemaking state of his, he made as comprehensive as possible.

Would you like to study a language, or a trade? he

inquired. I knew that this repayment was meant to be full and genuine. He would accept my staying home and at the same time he would truly believe that it didn't mean I was like the women.

I said to him that I would study what was in the books. I would do it on my own. These books, I wanted to make him understand, were not schoolbooks; and so I exaggerated their thickness, spreading my hands apart as far as they would go. He knew the books I meant. After all, he was the one who'd brought them to me from the book market where—though it was near his shop—he knew no one. These are books that are put onto bookshelves, not into school bookbags. Before he had moved them into the small hallway—that tight narrow space between the doors—I had been collecting them in my wardrobe, putting them together, one beside the next.

Lest he think that what was keeping me in the house was my laziness, I began each day exactly as I had the school day. I washed my face and got dressed, exactly as before, and sat down to read. I would start at eight o'clock, when school started. To be studying here as they were studying there. That was to placate him but also to reassure myself, because I still felt uneasy about being on my own and not at school. Like them, I would be beginning my studies at eight o'clock, and that lessened the distance I had put between myself and them. I would begin just as they did and at the very same time. And not in the room where I slept, nor on a sofa in the sitting room, but rather, in the hallway between the doors. Ever since moving into it, I had made this narrow passage into my own little classroom that had room enough to hold only me.

VII

Now, with the thirteenth year since our move
coming to a close, I know that what forced us to vacate the
city, leaving it completely empty, was simply that it no longer
had space enough to hold them. By *them* I mean the boys on
that school outing who, in the course of a single trip, managed to divide up and then redistribute the girls among themselves. *Them*: those who entertained themselves, on the bus,
blending dancing with laughter, mingling jokes and song. It
was as if there was too little time and so they tried to stretch
it by cramming in more activities. We vacated the city only
because it could no longer hold them. It was too cramped; its
narrow confines pressed in on them. It was too old for them,
and so they had carried themselves as if they were living in
their families' city and not in their own. It was like living in a
house furnished by your grandfather. It pressed in on them, it
was too old, and that is how they experienced it, as cramped
and ancient. All the while, everything they said or did in their
games served only to mark out the distance between themselves and everything around them, or to flaunt their sense of
how ahead of everyone else they were, how new and modern.
If the bus slowed to a crawl climbing the steep streets, they
sang about it and let the jokes fly. Yes, that is exactly what they

did, as if they were mocking the creaky backwardness of their own people and the slow pace of their folk's buses. If they danced it was for the sake of imitating certain styles of dance or to mimic dancing bodies too old to be seemly but who danced nevertheless. It was the same idea when they called things out the windows to passersby they spotted on the road, to make them—for these young lads' amusement—smile the dopey embarrassed smiles that were their response to greetings they could not understand.

No matter what they were doing, they would mock the situation they were in. The city had become too small for them—it was a city they regarded as behind or beneath them. This is how they were in the bus, on the trip where their joking and dancing united them. In the years to follow, when they broke apart to go their separate ways, the city hemmed them in even more as their lives grew ever more crowded and various, proliferating beyond their old familiar low-hanging horizon. Because of them we left the city. As enormous and spread out as it appeared to me, the part of it that I actually inhabited was a tiny space indeed: that little bit of the city that had room enough only for me. That passage between the three doors (one of them the door to the toilet whose odor my mother constantly feared would poison me), that hallway so well fortified from all outside commotion by the rooms that surrounded it, seeming to put vast distances between me and the outside world.

I chose to remain inside that narrow hallway while they tugged at their spaces, as if to lengthen and broaden them by pulling on the corners. Whenever my mother began to feel certain that there were too many books around me, she would ask in a voice whose tone she could not modulate: In the whole wide world, who but me would abandon a spacious room overlooking the street to spend his days here! And every time I handed my father a piece of paper on which I had written the title of a book, or maybe two, she would comment, in that high querulous voice of hers, that at least I should get out of the house for a bit. Or she would observe: The humidity in there would wear down even the strongest body. She meant, of course, that my fragile body was far more in need than most—indeed, it was the neediest—of exposure to clean, fresh air. But my father would take the piece of paper from me, delighted that I remained so attached to reading books. He would even—if it was morning and he was still in a good mood—ask me if this book whose title I had written down was one of those fat books that no one, in his view, ever read except judges and scholars of religion.

When my father brought me those books I always added them immediately to the ones already on the shelves as if the more books my library held, the surer I could be that eventually I would have lined the hallway walls with them, floor to ceiling. Now, after all these years have gone by, I know that what kept me shut in with my books was that they would take me back to the ancient times from which they hailed. I could read them and come to know those eras. In my mind I could even imagine myself to be living alongside the people of that time; it was easy, even without having actually experienced any of the events that occurred so long ago. As I read anecdotes, tales, vignettes of people's lives, dialogues, poems, and poetic duels, I could decide whether these were words on a page or real events in which real lives unfolded. Either way, I could be at a distance. I could play listener when I wanted to regard what I read as words, or I could play observer or witness when I decided to take them as things that actually happened to people of old. Listener or witness: just as I was in school, or on the outing, and whether standing or sitting. But always between me and what I saw there was an empty space, an extra space I made sure to leave in place, just in case I needed it. After all, they might well spill out of their own space; they might need more room. It was an empty space I would leave between them and me so that no one's arm would collide with me as its owner whipped around, suddenly making me a part of the circle even if only marginally so. It might put me inside the arena where their silly clowning created such a hubbub. I had to leave an empty space between them and me so that I could remain apart from their glee because I could not endure its intensity. Or I needed that space so that I would be able to flee at the point when I realized it would be better for me not to watch whatever was going on.

I had to keep a distance between them and me: the distance created by the empty seats in the bus or the space of the entire classroom. I had to sit at the very back of the classroom, my back to the wall, the students with their backs to me between myself and the teacher. At the very back of the class, in the last row and in the farthest seat. When the teacher pointed his finger in the air, asking himself which pupil he would single out, I would start playing the disappearing game. I'd shrink my sense of my own physical presence as much as I could, figuring that if he saw my reduced self he would pass right over it. I will not go back to school, I would say to my father after every occasion when I fell into their trap and found myself the butt of their stares. All it took was one of them saying something about me that he assumed only I would not understand. Or someone else imitating something about me behind my back, making all of them laugh and believing they were keeping the laughter among themselves. When I made a mistake writing two French words on the blackboard, the teacher asked me in front of all of them what kind of work I thought I could do if neglecting my homework got me expelled from school. He was about to go on, naming trades that required only hands and bodies, except that the students' heavy silence made him hesitate.

Each time, I would tell my father that I was not going back to school. I will read books on my own, I said to him that last time, and then he did keep me at home. Those books: I brought them along with me to this home of ours in this building that rises like a short fat tower. I am still reading them. These are the same books, on the same shelves; after my father left his shop in the old city I added no more. Taking them down from where I had put them, and reading them, it is as if I'm repeating the same class every year and I am never promoted to the next grade.

Those books: we line them up along the high shelves in anticipation that their time will come—their time to be read. We store them away carefully like household provisions that we must conserve. They grow old where they sit on the shelf because their expiration date begins to approach from the moment they're put up there. When we bring them down it's as though we're repeating ourselves, once again reading books we've already read and often disliked.

Those books: I had also begun to put them at a distance. Or perhaps they were putting me at a distance as they lay there on the table, open but face down. At night, as I lie sleepless in bed, the book on the table moves even farther away. The effort I calculate having to make to get up and go over to it is far more than the two or three steps separating the bed from the table. And by day I don't need my books, since I am waiting for her. As soon as we stand up from the table after our midday meal, I start waiting for her. As soon as I wash my hands and then don't know what to do next, I'm already waiting for her. My father tells me to take a break when he sees me coming out of my room so soon after going in. When he returns to the kitchen to stand next to my mother as she distributes the leftovers into their storage bowls and puts them away, I go to the window overlooking the sand track. It is two hours before she will appear. I know I won't see her there now. And I know that I might not be successful at catching sight of her when she is at the very top of the road so that I can watch her walk the entire distance. I might not, even if I spend the entire time between now and then pacing along that window, which is half open, half closed.

I spend a little time after our meal moving between my tiny space at the end of the apartment, and the empty bedroom whose window looks out on the road below. I pace back and forth, covering the breadth of the apartment, and I am only a little cautious. My father and mother, I know, have gone beyond a light doze into their heavy afternoon sleep, and I am free as I move about the house. I don't need to be more than minimally watchful where they are concerned. The sand track, warmed by the sun and dyed the intense yellow of sunshine, remains empty. Each time I glance out it is deserted. But she will come and I'll be here, from the moment she turns off the crowded main street to walk the length of the track, dragging her feet, showing how tired she is. Even from this distance I'll be able to see how her face is flushed and coated in a light sweat, which I see in my mind's eye covering her shoulders and upper arms and moistening her underarms with a dewy touch. I imagine the moisture of her exertions dampening her feet that the sand heats up inside her shoes. She won't remove her shoes until she's inside, at home, sitting in a chair she finds comfortable. Still not in any hurry, she'll take off her socks, white although soiled slightly from the dust and sand of the route she has to take. She'll put up her feet to wiggle her toes, observing them as they move, bare, free, released from their long hours in the prison of socks and shoes.

VIII

AND THEN, AT THE OPPOSITE window that looks out over the long stretch of sand, I wait for her to enter her room, just as I waited, and will wait, for her to leave it. But I will not actually see any of these things I'm waiting for. She won't come near the small area next to her window, since she has nothing to do in that space. I see no part of her entrance or exit, nothing of what she is doing in the meantime, but from the sounds she makes I'm able to make a very good guess. From the sound of her footfalls I can figure out which direction she has gone and where in the room she is right now. I can tell that she has pulled open one of the double doors to the wardrobe, and so I know she'll pull out one of the drawers inside. I can even hear the soft thud of her book falling onto her mattress and the swish of her blouse as she lifts it off her body and hangs it on the wardrobe doorknob.

And then the light switch—I hear its tiny click just as the light sails out her window and across the sand, making a long thin patch that is off-center from the light coming from my window. But that oblong of light creates no shadow of her on the sand, since she only moves around in the room's inner half. It's almost as if she believes that coming near the window means knowing that someone is surely standing there at the other edge of the sand and will see her. Or perhaps she stays in that part of the room because she's in a hurry and wants to stay near the door. As for me, waiting overhead, I figure she does not even know I'm here. She doesn't know about me. If she did know about me, she would not let these irritable phrases—these angry, sharp words—slip from her mouth. No, not if she knew I was here, immediately above her window. Not those words, which are very nearly swear words and which come out of her whenever something slows her down or she can't find what she's looking for. She does not know about me. The light in my room going out just now does not alert her to anything at all because a few moments ago, there in her room, she didn't notice that my light was on. Or she didn't realize the light up here had been turned on after it was off. She would have to be slower and more deliberate in her movements, she would need to be calmer, for her to be able to work her brain over a sound she hears or a light she sees. A person in as much of a hurry as she is—indeed, any person her age—does not take shadow created by light falling from the window above to mean that someone is there behind the window. Her head is not occupied with what she sees or hears, because it's just following her body in its abrupt changes of course, as if a reverse current has suddenly charged through it and driven it back from the direction in which it was heading.

This body of hers: hardly has it come into the room before it goes out. Only a moment or two, no more; and in those moments it's as if I'm actually seeing it, this body of hers. When the drawer opens I can practically see that form bending over it, and as the wardrobe door clicks firmly shut it's as if I'm watching this body leaning forward ever so slightly to heave the door into place. I sit waiting for it, preparing myself to get up from my chair, to go over to the windowsill and hang my head and shoulders out if I sense that the charge governing it will send it over to where I can see it. Really see it.

That evening I realized it was going to happen. Every time she came into the room she spent more time in it than usual. Her steps were slow and few, and everything she touched or looked at stopped her. When she opened the wardrobe door and then I heard no further sound, I said to myself, She is looking at herself in the mirror right now. Then I had the thought that perhaps she had begun revealing parts of herself to the mirror. This idea dawned on me when she nearly ran out of the room, or at least as far as the door, as if she were making certain no one had come anywhere near the door, which she had mistakenly left open. She would return, though. After all, she had not shut the wardrobe door, nor had she turned off the light. So I knew that she would return. And that it was going to happen. Leaning over my windowsill, angling my head and shoulders down, I would see her.

She did not stay long in the interior of the apartment where the sitting room was. When she was once again in the room, directly below me, she closed the door and went immediately back to the mirror. It must be a mirror that rose as high as the wardrobe door itself, so high that a person standing at it would be invisible to the emptiness there near the sweep of sand. She is concealed by the long slender rectangle formed by the closed door of the room and the wardrobe door opposite it, the two creating a sort of narrow hallway. Even I, watching and listening so attentively above, sensed that she was perfectly hidden there. Only my imagination could help me know what she was doing. For she had removed her body from the space commanded by her open window, from where she sent a part of it outward, carried by air and light, into the

63

boundless emptiness that I share with her. All I could do was imagine her, try to fix her in a series of overlapping images that crowded in on each other only to erase one another as if, hidden there, she had severed every gesture, every sign or indication, by which I might have been able (just possibly) to reach her.

On that particular evening however, standing in front of the mirror would not be enough for her. It seemed as though something in her had awakened suddenly and—even in such a short interval—had transformed her. Hanging over the window ledge, I would wait for her to appear below me, to stand here where I can see, revealing now this part of her body and now that one to the outside where she knows there is no one. If this is what she is doing then it is a way of taking another step forward in accepting and responding to the abrupt change that has come over her.

This is what I want and do not want at the same time. I would love to see the bare skin of her shoulders as close as this but I am not happy with the thought that she is exposing herself bare-shouldered to the wide-open space beyond the windows as if to challenge someone out there to see her. Nor do I like the idea of her standing hidden behind the wardrobe mirror, where only she can see herself and where, I imagine, some internal urge is locked in a quarrel with some other instinct, one part of her trying to entice the other out of its accustomed state. This is what I do not want because it causes her to know her body. I want her body to stay small and child-like, unconscious of itself, knocking into everything around it haphazardly the way a child's body does, as when she walks in the morning to the end of the sand track. I love to see her then, her heavy school bag swaying, striking her between the shoulders so that she jerks forward, still grumbling because someone woke her up from a deep sleep. I desperately want to be the one—the only one—who will bring something un-childlike from her body, a body that returns sweaty and ex-hausted from school. I want her to be ignorant of her body, unaware of its forces. Only then—and if there were to hap-pen between us what normally happens between neighbors who have lived near each other for a long time—can I put my hand on her arm and invite her to come in. Then my hand could go to her face, wiping off a muddy or oily splotch left by the school bus, and she would believe the only rea-son I touched her was to wipe away the dirty spot. I would see her bare feet as she padded through the house, with me there, nearby, so close I can muse about reaching out a hand and touching those little feet, just like that, naturally, as if I'm brushing off the dust that clings to them. Maybe I could reach out and catch hold of one foot, from the inside, from that inner arch that slopes down to the bottom of her foot. If the people sitting with us were to leave, if she were the only one still there, alone, sitting with me, that is what I would do.

On this particular evening as I lean against the window ledge and hang down over it, I know that she will come close to where I can see her and not just the shadow of her. She will come so near that she'll be exactly beneath me, I know it. She'll stand in front of the open square of the window, poised there exactly as she stood in front of the mirror. She will think she's risking nothing. She's only offering what was in the mir-ror to onlookers she creates in her mind. That's what she will do. The same way she stood before the mirror, that's how she will stand now, but in front of that open square of the window. And so from where I am, immediately overhead, I will see her; when she comes over here I will see her and she'll be just as she was there, showing her self to herself in the mirror.

Behind me, the light in my room is out. There is no light to create a shadow of me across the sand that lies so close beneath us. I can wait like this for hours, assured that no one sees me or knows that I'm here. But I will not need to wait very long. Although she has come away from where she stood, there below, she has left the wardrobe door open. Did she go over to her bed, perhaps? Or maybe she walked toward a table that I haven't realized was there, near the bed. And then . . . but here she is now, coming back this way: something has moved in the light descending from her room. It's not her shadow; it's merely the phantom image of her movement inside the room.

She will come.

She has come closer; she has walked toward the window. What was a formless movement playing on the sand, a flickering of the light, is now a real and solid image. She is coming, now; her shadow arrives. In the instant when her shadow becomes complete out on the sand she appears behind it; and I, in that selfsame moment, have prepared myself to see her appear, fully and truly appear. Her golden hair is combed and wound in the way of older women. Farther down, below her neck whose nakedness seems (from the back) so elongated, she wears nothing but a child's sleeveless cotton undershirt that reveals the rounding of her small breasts, not yet fully developed. She wears a shirt worn not to be seen but only to lie beneath other clothes. And the breasts beneath it—these small breasts that I want only to pass my hands over, for desire has not yet reached them, has not arrived to touch them. Yes, this is what I want: I am he who desires the body whom desire has not yet caught.

IX

I CAN TELL BY LOOKING into my father's eyes how weak his vision has become. My father's eyes: or rather, what I see is the filmy layer that has smeared across the pupils, and which at first had looked like a thinly delicate transparent nylon skin. But it was visible even then; and I would always imagine a skilled hand treating it by peeling it carefully off the surface of the eye. I was still in school then. I would speculate that through his eyes all objects were seen as if behind a wafer-thin, watery screen. As time went on—for the film over his eyes first appeared when he still had the shop—the screen grew dirty. The nylon skin went grayish as if (it appeared to me) it had thickened and grown slightly heavier and rougher. My father's gaze from behind it seemed changed—even imprisoned—by it; a gaze strangled, like a lung barely able to breathe because there is too little air outside.

By looking into those eyes I could register the degree to which his eyesight had left him. Some time after we moved to this place of ours my father began to expand the circle in the air inside of which he set his shop; then he would let his finger drop to the point he judged as the center of the circle. Is that where our shop is? he would ask, making it sound like an earnest question, even if he didn't seem to care much about what the response would be. The colossus of dust rising from a felled building would not be visible to him until it was very high, and then it would appear to him suddenly as a dirty cloud in the intensely blue sky.

Where have they gotten to now? he would ask, getting me to describe for him what I could see of their work down there. When I answered that they were working at the lowest edge on the eastern side of the city he would start naming names, some of which I didn't know. You mean Bukhari Rise, he would say, identifying the spot I had described. Or are they in the Mansions Quarter? He wanted to sound as though he knew every inch of that territory. So, what are they working at down there? he would ask me—yet again. I would have to tell him what the bulldozers and trucks I could see were doing, where they were stopping before they converged into one mass, performing some task that I could not make out.

They're still knocking down buildings, I would tell him. Or I would say that they were close to finishing in this district, since only a few buildings still remained for them to knock down.

As I described what I saw he would begin to sketch outlines, plans for what they ought to do as they worked there. They will join up the Nouriyya souq and the Amir mosque, he would declare, since they're destroying what's left of the buildings between them. Or he would say that it would have been better for them to begin with the structures at the edge of the souq so they could clear a path for themselves from there to the sea. When this enthusiasm for giving advice and correcting errors and reworking plans got a firm hold on him, he would suddenly turn to me and remark of my mother (who was staring at the little stitches her needles made) that she was working with wool in the height of summer. She would hear him, but rather than answer she would look at me with a sly smile as if to remind me that we had a secret understanding, knowing to keep quiet about his tiresome drivel. That will put burns on your hands, he would announce as he turned to her, wanting to put a stop to the collusion he'd noticed between us, and to sweep it away altogether.

It comforts her to work her hands by moving them in those tiny and regular movements. The routine diverts her. A little upward movement with one hand, ending in a knot that her other hand flies up to conceal. As her hand sweeps upward she senses herself in a light and cheery mood, the way little girls feel when they amuse themselves by chewing gum. In the years since our move, my mother grew used to having us stay at home and she began shifting from one mode to another throughout the long day. Sitting down in the late afternoon, hair and clothes patted into place, she had the air of having just returned from somewhere else. Or she looked as though she had been readying herself to receive guests whom she knew would not show up. My father thought that this daily ritual she had, of sitting like this in her good clothes, demonstrated that she was empty-headed. She just went on smiling for no apparent reason—since nothing called for a smile—and she seemed so like a child, humming to herself in a low and light voice or staring at the space between the needles as if to toy with the stitch that had slipped between them. He thought she was featherbrained and childish, sitting there just so in the late afternoon, but he didn't say anything about it or even hint at it. It showed, though, in the way he looked at her and then turned away like someone who has seen something embarrassing. Or he would keep his gaze fixed on her face, looking at her silently as though reminding himself of something.

But the way I saw it, of the three of us she was the only one who actually might be capable of receiving a guest who just might come to visit us. What did not please my father about her pose did please me. Or, it began to please me once I started to think that she must go down to their home—down there, just below us—to visit them. There, in their sitting room or on their balcony, she would look fresh and well put together. Down there, they would see her meaningless smile as a sign of how pleased she felt about them and how delighted she was to be among them.

Something about the way we live here has to change, I said, standing up and leaning on the balcony railing. I wasn't speaking to anyone in particular but my father looked at me, craning his head forward and even projecting his ears as though to make certain he missed none of the words he expected me to add to what he'd just heard. As for my mother, she raised her eyes to me but only so she could say that this life of ours was one that no one could bear. She went on looking at me—they were both staring at me—as if urging me on to complete what I had begun. I said to them that I must go to work, which doubled their astonishment.

Now this was something for which neither of them could have any rejoinder. My mother went back to her needles, rescuing herself from any chance that she might say something she'd regret later. But I know she had been waiting. She'd been waiting not simply to hear me say this, but indeed for me to do it. We're living off our savings and we're eating them up, she'd frequently said to my father, for whom work was no longer possible. But time had passed since I had heard her say it. No doubt by now we had eaten up quite a lot of the savings that would have allowed my father to open a new shop.

What work will you do? my father asked me, adopting an

exaggeratedly serious look on his face. I'll work at something I'm capable of doing, I responded, making him so uncomfortable that his face froze into that solemn expression.

Something about the way we live here has to change, I said turning toward my mother. I had calculated that all she would need to take the first step was for someone to say something about it. She was gratified to find me singling her out rather than my father and was on the verge of saying so, were it not for the critical position in which she found herself, which she tried to hide by bringing the tiny stitches closer to her eyes and seeming to stare at them. All she needed was one little gesture to make her feel her distinction from the others who lived here, even though she seemed completely unaware of how to act appropriately for a woman of her age. She so loved to exhibit that femininity of hers. I supposed that she was imitating the emotions of girls who have not yet matured. That's why she would smile to herself like that, in those moments in the late afternoon, and why she put her hair up in styles that were only suited for young girls.

But she will know how to act when they open the doors to their home and find her there, expecting to visit them. Once inside, she'll know how to behave when they ask her to sit down in what I imagine is their sitting room. It is directly below the large room my family had designated for me. They'll be happy with her there, and she will not allow their time together to pass slowly and tediously. The way she sits with us, with me and my father, so well put together and smiling to herself, I think, is simply practice for the possibility that she will receive visitors who might come to our door, or that she might visit people who will welcome her into their homes. She will not annoy them there, in their sitting room above which rises the window I stand behind in order to watch the one for whom I wait, standing motionless, in expectation of her departure for school or her return from it. I might not hear anything of what they say; it will be only a guess, thinking about what my mother will do when she stands there ready to meet her just coming out of her room, and then when she looks hard at her, wanting to really see her, right there in front of her, so very close.

X

THE OFFICES OF THE MAGAZINES that my father bought me when we were still in the old city are no longer where they're supposed to be either, at the addresses written inside each issue. The editors left, just like the shopkeepers my father knew. Sitting here in our home, I think about them. They must have moved to offices in the new parts of town, I think, offices of no more than one room or perhaps two. Not all of them moved, since the displacement of an entire city has to mean that many things are overlooked, and then abandoned. The magazines in my library—magazines that haven't been updated with a new issue since our move here—I think of as uniformly old, as if I bought them all in the same moment. When I hoist these bundles from the shelves to carry them over to the table, I see that they've aged the books sitting next to them: these books that have not had a single volume added to their number either, ever since our move. When we first moved, when I could have bought books because we were still living off what my father called *the expense account*, I felt I already had enough of them. Some were still new then. Or they were new in my library, since for us a book is deemed new according to the moment we possess it and not the date it was written. When we moved I said I would read from what

73

I already had around me, echoing the condition of the prisoner who—every time I think of sitting down to read—I find myself longing to impersonate: both in the cramped, narrow space he inhabits and in his careful hoarding of his belongings, among them books that he has no choice but to read there in his tiny prison cell, word by word, over and over.

But now I know (so long after our move) that the books aging on our shelves are a burden to read. Every time I get to that point—the moment of actually starting to read one of them—it's as if it's already a question of rereading it, even though the most I've ever done is to leaf through a few pages. I thought that in order to begin doing work I would know how to do (as I suggested to my father and mother on the balcony late in the afternoon), I must get to know something new I could bring to it, something new I would only get from books in bookshops and not from those in my library. Or I had to see what the magazines were doing now, after I had been cut off from them for all these years. This time, though, I am the one who must go out. Not my father, who, since ceasing his reconnaissance tours around the neighborhoods, goes only to the very nearest shops, those that are no distance at all from the top of the sand track.

My father, returning tired and sometimes completely exhausted from these tours of his, would tell my mother that he found it amazing to see how people were getting on with their lives as if nothing had befallen them and none of their circumstances had changed. Like an ant, he would say, squeezing two fingers together as if to pick up a tiny ant and move it from one spot where it had been creeping along to another. Like an ant, he would say to my mother, an ant who starts crawling immediately and in the very same direction the minute we put it back on the ground. By this time he and my mother had reached a point where they were beginning to sense that we had waited too long to open a new business out there in one of the city quarters where my father took his long walks. That's why my mother did not comment but only gave him that silent gaze meaning she had already warned him that he must work, and it must happen soon. Then he stopped going on those long walks of his through the new neighborhoods. The small makeshift shops erected hastily in building entryways or beneath staircases had become real shops now, even if they had only tiny storefronts or were set far back from the street. During his final walks through those neighborhoods and among those shops, my father began to view them as if, together with the structures surrounding and towering over them, they had filled in all the emptiness. They had not left the tiniest morsel of empty space for anyone.

Like ants, they start again from where you set them down, my father would say before declaring that when he went out again he would not go any farther than was necessary to buy meat and vegetables for the household. In our daily life we no longer needed anything more than that, as long as we didn't break anything that would require going out for a repair. He no longer went beyond the shops that started up just as he turned off onto the street at the top of the sand track. It was a matter of three or four shops among which he hovered as he collected the few things that we truly needed. He would return quickly, so that he could rapidly pull them out of the bags, one after another, as if revealing to my mother gifts she had not expected. His mission would not be truly complete until he had counted the items he had set down, announcing each one by name and finally asking himself whether he had forgotten anything. Only then was his errand finished: or his journey, for he would let out the deep groan of a person whose energy has been completely spent, and would begin looking around to see what he should do first to relieve his tired body in the restfulness of home.

It would be my task now to go out, scrutinizing the shops and the signs above them as soon as my feet met the tar of the street. Despite my knowing that no other course of action would be of any use, I contemplated the idea of an interval between my decision to go out and actually going out. A short time I could convince myself I needed in order to get ready for the streets I would walk, to learn something about them before actually heading down into them. A time of rest before going out, or a time of waiting; it was nothing more, since I already knew (sitting and waiting there at home) that nothing would help guide me to the right thoroughfares or the small streets I needed. Yes, an interval of rest and of waiting; in any case, I could train my body or prepare it for walking along among all the others walking the streets—walking that my body had experienced before, movement that my body had known, long ago.

XI

FROM THE WINDOW OF MY room, and from the kitchen window and also the balcony if I choose to go out there, I can see her when she comes out to join the two of them where they've decided to sit down. They will not be far away, probably because they got tired of walking across the sand. Their feet will have sunk into it deep enough so that each time they tried to take a step that foot would feel trapped. Or perhaps they didn't go far because they wanted to stay within reach of any voices that might call out from their homes in the building. As nearby as they were, though, it looked as if they had prepared themselves for a lengthy excursion. My mother had spread out a blanket over the sand. The other woman had carried out an enormous umbrella that she anchored in the ground. Then they sat down, resting from the walk to their chosen spot and exposing their faces to the breeze gently batting at them—the very same puffs of air that would have reached them on the balcony of either apartment.

And from either balcony they could have enjoyed the very same view they now sat facing. They had even chosen to turn their faces—together—to that vista rather than sit down facing each other so that whichever one was talking could see the other. It seemed that the preferred object of their stares was not the old city at the farthest point of the panorama that lay before them, but rather, the emptiness of the wide abyss that separated them from it.

They loved to go out by themselves. They would not be expecting to see anyone but her; and anyway, they would have gone out before she could show up to join them, so that the first phase of the excursion would be entirely an outing of the older women on their own. The two of them could gab as they wished and sit exactly as they pleased, since they could be sure that no one would suddenly appear from the other direction where the sand rises in small dunes. The couple living on the ground floor would not appear from behind the shutters that they never opened except to water the greenery just below.

Whatever the circumstances, the pair of them would be taking full advantage of their little excursion, stretching their legs out in front of them, calculating the likelihood that my eyes and my father's eyes might be on them. Perhaps one of us would glance out through a window or from the balcony, not because either of us was curious but out of sheer boredom, as the women surely knew. My father, though, seemed absolutely delighted as he declared—after checking to make certain that they really were sitting together out there—that today the two of us would lunch alone. Already on his way to the kitchen and ready to manage lunch on his own, he would turn back to ask me what dish I was longing for, so that he could make it for me.

In the past few days—ever since my mother had begun going down to their apartment—he had avoided looking at her except when he was trying to work out why her enthusiasm for making visits gave her such a juvenile demeanor. When she was down there with them he behaved as though he and I were living completely alone in the house. Shall I boil you some water for tea? he would ask; or he would announce, from the other side of my closed door, that he would be on the balcony and I must raise my voice if I wanted anything from him. What would you like to eat today? he would ask me, rubbing his hands together in preparation for putting them to work.

She had not yet left the building. The two women sat alone, their legs extended toward the vast emptiness that held their gaze. I was always able to see her the moment she rounded the building toward the rear and stood exactly below me for a moment before setting out across the sand. Or I would catch a glimpse of her from the stairwell in the moment when she opened her front door and stepped out. At that moment she would suddenly be much closer to me, since this building, with its narrow passageways and half-walls that are meant to screen us from each other, protects her from knowledge of many things. But that very fact might mean she would be more sensitive to my presence, as I hid there, hunched over close by, with just the top of my head visible above the low wall around the stairs. When my mother returned from her first visit she said they knew more about us than we knew about them. Immediately she realized what I might be thinking. She surmised that I might be suspicious that they had tried to learn more about me. Quickly she added that they knew the nature of my father's work in the old city.

Do they know where our shop was? my father asked her, elbowing himself into the conversation though he had clearly intended to appear uninterested, looking in every other direction but at her, studiously self absorbed.

Outside, the pair of them sat there doing nothing more than resting their legs and staring at the broad emptiness in front of them. They gave no sign of precisely how they had planned to enjoy themselves in making an elaborate excursion out of the building. Everything they had carried out there was in exactly the same position where they had first set it all down. From the window of my room—through the slit I had left open—I could see them gazing fixedly, as if they were expecting someone to come and rescue them from the silence into which they had fallen soon after arranging themselves out there. The way toward them across the sand remained empty, though. They took turns scrutinizing it, but they had the air of looking for something that was increasingly unlikely to happen. She had not even opened the window to her room, nor had she appeared at the kitchen window that looked out on the two of them where they sat below. Turning to look, her mother found no one to wave to. Probably, I thought, *she* liked having the house all to herself and decided to stay inside. There among the rooms, doors flung wide, she could move around however she liked. She could be as free within those spacious, empty rooms as she would normally be in her bathroom. She could expose her naked body, fully revealed, to the many mirrors in the apartment and not merely to the one that hung on her wardrobe.

And so she is not immediately below me; she is not in her own room. She is moving around. She roves through the apartment: through this home that has been emptied for her. Not even I can pinpoint where she might be right now, in what room she's standing, which way she'll move next. At the window of my room, cracked open slightly, I begin to think that like the two women I am also waiting for an event that will not take place. I stand here motionless as time runs on: but it only does so down there, below me, in a space that begins behind my back and spreads out to fill their home. No, time does not move on here. Not here at the window where I stand. Time has stopped here. The women, too: they are still sitting there, brooding. The path leading to them is still and silent too; and there is no sign that it expects anything to reverse its mute emptiness. I do not know what to do. It's useless to leave my room hoping to track her footsteps through the spaces of her home. I will not hear the sound of her bare and slightly sticky feet slowly disengaging as she pads across the glinting tiles. Time no longer passes here, not at the window. The time I have come to wait for. I wait for time to start its passage again. I wait for my father's light, cautious knock on my door and then his voice asking me, Shall I boil you some water for tea? Would you like a glass of water? Cold water?

I wait for my father to arrive, even if it's just for the sake of answering him that I don't want anything at all. Or I think about coming out of my room and going into the kitchen; perhaps by the time I reach the kitchen window I'll be able to see some sort of change in the tableau they've made out there. Or I wait for the two women—if they see me over here behind the window—to wave to me. My mother might even call out to me loudly enough that, below me, *she* will hear it. This will finally animate the scene out there, because once it happens the two women will know it's time to begin wrapping up their outing. Likewise, if my mother's voice reaches her—there below where she moves through the house—perhaps she will stop wandering among the rooms and stopping at every mirror.

Then she will return to the spot where she left her clothes thrown on the floor opposite the first mirror that captured her. And so, for me to stand at the open kitchen window will put time into motion—this time that at present is fractured among different locations, each isolated from the others. And so I must go there, I must: I will leave the window behind which I conceal myself and walk toward the door that I was certain my father would head for as soon as he heard the small sound it makes as it opens. As I lessened the distance between myself and the floors below, I let that sound reverberate as if I were summoning my father toward it, or at least, by making it as if I were pinpointing his position in the house. But as I went out into the hallway I heard no sound of him coming, nor did I see him standing in the doorway to the kitchen looking at me inquiringly to find out what I wanted. It seemed as if no sound made by any of the doors in our house had reached him. Since I had come from my room to the kitchen without hearing anything from him, I was certain that he was in his room, asleep at that early point in the day. All I would have to do was to stand behind the open kitchen window. All I would have to do was to show myself to them at the center of the window and then step back from it before I appeared again, as if I had been here in the kitchen all along, absorbed in an ordinary task that kept me busy.

From the kitchen window the spectacle they presented had not changed. Together, the two of them stared at the emptiness in front of them as if something were happening there. But they would turn to where I stood, or one of them would, catching sight of me. If together they waved to me I would behave as if I were preoccupied with something else and didn't see them waving. That's what I would do, so that my mother would call out to me. And maybe the woman would give her some help: together their voices would carry, and she would hear that from wherever she was. Once all of this had happened I would have to quickly go to the stairs to wait for her, hidden behind the balustrade. I must see her from the very first step she takes out of the apartment, for very little time will have passed since she was moving among the mirrors and looking at her body naked and fully revealed. When she appears in the doorway she will have just quickly thrown her dress on over her body, which will still be feverishly hot. From behind the balustrade I will see her while she is still in her state of confused excitement. Indeed, when she appears she'll be in more disarray than she was in there, in front of the mirrors, still trying to stop the thing that was welling up inside of her like warm and thrusting waves.

XII

THEY BEGAN TO WAVE AT me from where they sat on
the sand, having seen me behind the kitchen window. Then
they began to call out to me in unison, from that distance, to
come and join them. The woman was raising her hand repeatedly and waving it around in my direction, even though
I supposed she could not see me clearly. She knew of me;
and sitting there with my mother, she had learned more
about me, since no doubt when the two of them sat down
and immediately began jabbering they were focusing on me.
It might have been over very quickly, with just a few passing
questions that my mother answered rapidly and without any
deliberation or even shifting in her seat. Come . . . come . . .
the woman's hand was saying, sweeping from the direction
where I stood to dip toward her own body, a gesture to bring
me to her side. When the two of them stopped calling and
waving I left the kitchen empty, since there was no need now
for them to see me there. In his room, its door left open, my
father was stretched out on his bed, dozing. He lay on top of
the bedcovers that he had left made up beneath him. Still, I
thought that I wouldn't be able to behave freely in the house.
Lying down on top of the made bed was a way of keeping
himself ready to rise immediately if my voice came to him or

if he should sense that it was time to ask me if I wanted anything. I slowly stepped back from where, in the sitting room, I was looking in at him. As I put distance between myself and his open door, I was aware that although he seemed to be submerged in sleep he would awaken at the slightest sound or movement. I retreated to my room and the mirror hanging so high on the wall that to see my face and chest in it I had to stand on the edge of the bed that was positioned directly below it. I figured I should do this before I went out there: out to the balustrade that gives me the protection of a short wall. The sound of the bolt when I opened the door was too faint for my father to hear as long as he was still dozing. But, just as I stepped outside I heard the sound of her steps below, her last swift steps bringing her to the entryway of the building, and I was only able to see her for a fleeting moment.

When I got back to the window in my room she was just stepping onto the sand. She was below me and the sand slowed her progress, exasperating her every time she had to raise her feet that had sunk into it. She even seemed on guard against the sand rising farther, for I could see her lifting the legs of her trousers, revealing just a tiny strip of white flesh that I figured wouldn't even be visible once she had gone a bit farther. Her next steps only added to her fatigue and irritation. As she poked her foot sharply into the sand she had the look of doggedly resisting something or someone while being just as stubbornly resolved to obey. Her movements disturbed her thick braid, which swung out across her shoulders, highlighting the nakedness of her neck and tracing a broad semicircle high on her back.

It did nothing to dispel her irritation that when they saw her the two women began waving at her, or that they had twisted round to stare in her direction while remaining seated with their legs poking out in front of them. It seemed the pair of them would stay like that, as if to encourage her on her way over to them. Once she had gotten close, her mother stretched out both arms to her in a festively welcoming gesture. The nearer she came the more enchanted my mother seemed; it looked to me as if in her bedazzled staring my mother had forgotten about the niceties of welcoming her.

She was already standing behind the two of them in the space between where they still sat when I became aware of my father standing behind me, about to take a step in from the doorway to my room. Both of us looked as if we'd been caught out by the other one, for we were each startled and confused, each of us waiting for the other to say something. His hand rose to point at the door, wanting me to understand that I had left it open; and then he said, to excuse his coming up behind me like this, that sleep had overtaken him and he thought I might need something that he could get for me. He hadn't taken even one more step into the room. He kept his diseased eyes fixed on my face as if to keep them from falling on anything but me. I could tell that he was suspicious of my standing there hiding behind the window, looking out through a narrow crack. Leaving me where I was, he turned to go, and I knew that he would head directly to the kitchen window to see for himself what it was that had led me to stand there hidden like that, looking surreptitiously out of the window. Even if he stared at them, he would not see them clearly, but neither would he return to ask me if what he saw was accurate. I turned back to my window and closed my eyes as if to make them dim-sighted. I began to imagine what he might be able to see of the women. Standing there, she appeared as a shadow or a ghost. I quickly brought that shape into focus, out of its haziness, to appear to me clearly once again. Suddenly I realized that my father had probably thought I was spying on the other woman. I immediately turned my eyes to her legs that remained splayed out in front of her. He would not see her clearly from where he was standing and exposing himself to their view. He would not even know which of the two women sitting there was my mother; he would not ask me about that either, since asking would return us to our state of embarrassment. Remaining there, staring, he would make his own guesses. He would go on standing there staring at all of them, and perhaps, if he felt his standing there, directly in their line of vision, had gone on too long, he would shift sideways to stand at one edge of the window as I did, or he would close the outer, wooden panel. But he would go on staring in that direction, wanting to recognize what it was about the way the woman sat, or what it was about her body, that would call for hiding oneself to spy from behind a closed window. He would go on looking until he might discover it, doing it for my sake and not his own. Throughout the many years that have passed since I reached an age he calculated to be my adolescence he has not stopped asking himself—and asking my mother as well—whether I have matured like other boys. From among the huge sacks in his shop whose edges he would roll back, or as he filled the small sacks with the contents of the large ones, he would look at me as a woman passed in front of us and I would know, even with my back turned to him, that he was staring at me. I could be certain that once he was back at home he would be asking my mother: Have you seen anything? Are there any signs you've been able to see?

He would go on staring at them out there. At the woman seated on the sand, and not at her daughter who might as well have been outside his field of vision. He would look only at

88

the two women who sat there, ignoring her—she who now stood apart from them almost at the edge of the steep and perilous downward slope to the chasm that divides us from the old city. She moves closer to the edge, cautiously, to examine the slope itself and to make out from there the bottom point where it ends. No doubt the two women were beginning to warn her away from the rim just as she took two steps toward it. Here is her mother now, stretching out an arm that will not be long enough to reach her at that distance, as though the force of that single gesture would bring her daughter back from the edge.

This time my father knocked on the door, lightly and slowly. Giving me a little time before he opened it, he said he would begin to heat up our lunch now, if I wished him to. The window was as nearly closed now as it had been when he left me. He tried to give a quick glance in its direction but it wasn't fast enough, and then—his hand still gripping the doorknob—he asked whether I was hungry yet. When I responded by saying that he could go ahead and eat if he wanted to, it was as if what I really wanted was for him to close my door and leave me alone. First my mother's leaving the house had disturbed him, and now I was giving him further cause for annoyance. Seeing me spying from behind the shutters had placed him in a dilemma he could not resolve by himself. He needed someone at his side, not simply to tell him whether what he thought he saw was really there, but also to help him deal with the thoughts he was having. Have you noticed anything yet? he would have said to my mother if she had not been out there sitting next to the woman whose shape he could not make out at all. You wash his clothes, he would have added, bringing his mouth close to her ear, his persistent questioning all but plastering him to her, keeping him close behind whenever she turned or took a step. In his bed, then? he would ask. Right now he desperately needed my mother's presence. Yes, her going out had disturbed him and now her absence annoyed him and made him anxious. He will not be able to stand still. He'll move constantly between the kitchen and the door to my room, like this, waiting for something to come to him, from whatever direction it might arrive.

She was still standing at the edge of the slope, though she had turned away from it to look toward the women, who seemed to be talking to her. Out there on the sand where the pair of them sat close to the edge, she couldn't be alone. She could not stand at a distance by herself and be truly apart, for there was nothing out there she could stand behind or with which she might shade herself. No wall, no tree; and so she would keep standing there—in front of them, behind them, it didn't matter—and she would have nothing to amuse herself with, there at the outer reaches of the sand. The swelling mounds rising slightly above the flat surface were not high enough to hide anything, or even to separate one stretch from another. It wouldn't be long before my father would return to my door, knocking lightly again. He would tell me he was waiting for me and wouldn't eat lunch without me. I thought about going out and telling him to eat his lunch alone if he was hungry so that I wouldn't have to wait for his knock.

He was standing at the threshold between the kitchen and the hallway that leads to my room, confused. He hesitated between completing his route toward me and returning to the kitchen, which he had not yet fully left. Realizing that I was about to return immediately to my room, he said that he wouldn't eat lunch either. But he couldn't hide his irritation, with me and with my mother whose excursion seemed to signal that her sole aim was to punish him by leaving him alone. Turning toward his own room, he told me that I could eat when I felt like it.

Back in my room, I began making the preparations that one makes before going out. I hoisted myself up toward the mirror again, but this time just to see my face in it. My part was still razor-straight and required only a pat into place, and then a stroke across my eyebrows beneath, like so, and everything was in its proper place. As for my clothes, I could see them well enough without the mirror. I had only to unbutton and rebutton, undo the belt and fasten it again. It all took only a few moments and then I was ready. Prepared. I might go out; I might even go out, to where they all sat, at the exact moment when I felt absolutely certain that I must be there. The three of them would see me, fully and completely, as soon as I put my foot down on the sand. I will move forward across the sand, step by step, advancing straight toward them. Striding determinedly and confidently toward them, I'll show myself to them. And all the while they will be looking at me, turning fully in my direction. They will not take their eyes off me as I advance, step by step. As they stare at me, perhaps they'll have the air of spectators observing a man who plunges forward to embark on an adventure before a silent, wary audience that wonders how far he'll actually go. Maybe I can go out there to them at the moment I am convinced that it's my best move. I'll keep walking toward them over the sand, step by step, until I reach the little patch of ground where they have united. I will get there. I will stand among them all. I will not say anything once I'm there among them. That will be perfectly natural, since they'll know I need to pause for a few moments of rest after my journey.

XIII

I HAD COME OUT BY myself, even though my father said I had to allow him to accompany me, especially on this first excursion. He went on insisting until I was actually out the door. On the staircase landing behind the balustrade the two of them stood together, he and my mother, saying goodbye to me and watching my every step as I descended. From the window of their bedroom, to which they quickly moved, they continued to watch me walk up the sand track. It occurred to me that even as they stood there together at the window my mother would still be saying to him that it would indeed be best if he went with me. The same firm gait that I had resolved to use for going out to *them* where they sat was carrying me not there but rather here, along the route toward the crowds. I heard the sound of the wind coming up from below, whirling and coming in waves as if opposing currents of wind tussled and tossed in the steep, empty chasm leading to the old city. I knew that as I advanced, leaving most of the road behind me, no trace of that sound would follow once I got there, for the commotion and loud voices of the crowds would replace it.

I did allow my father to sketch out streets and intersections, his hands slicing wildly through the air. He began following routes in his head that he soon lost track of, returning to a beginning point that he didn't bother to explain to me. He seemed to be remembering the roads for himself, and meanwhile from behind him my mother gestured to me not to pay him any heed. At one point it seemed he had fallen into the trap of his own maze and no longer knew how to get out of it; probably, in any case, he said to me, they have made many changes to the streets. He no longer knew what was there beyond the intersecting streets that defined the entrance to the sand track. I told him I would ask the passersby and get directions from them. Leave him alone . . . let him go, my mother began saying to him—my mother whose enthusiasm for visits and outings had given her a new love for risks and ventures out. He won't get lost, she said, turning away as she tossed me a playful, slightly challenging look—as if she were giving me a little hint that she had some particular and special bit of knowledge about me.

Getting to the street at the end of the sand track was easy. But as soon as I stepped onto it I knew I had come out a bit too early. The shops on either side of the street held no one but their proprietors, busy readying them to receive customers. I wasn't forced to walk among the crowds; the residents of the apartments, or so I guessed, were still at home. I had come out early and this was better for me since it meant that only a handful of people would see me. On either side of the narrow street—the first one after the sand track—I got the feeling that the only reason anyone had come down to their shop so early was to seek a little distraction. Despite the lack of crowds I didn't slow my pace or glance into a single shop, or when I got near a shop, I did not look directly at the man inside. I could only look from a distance, three or four shops ahead, for instance at that man whom I could see bent over his crates. Moving forward, I needed to preserve a similar distance, always gazing three or four shops ahead.

That way my eyes would never meet the gaze of others I happened to encounter on the street or in the shops, and so my eyes could wander over them when they were not looking at me. And that way, I could leave someone behind when I was still walking by his shop. It was best for me to stare straight ahead, three or four shops in front of me. A passing glance, never a stare, and thus I would seem occupied with matters my head was busily turning over and not with what I saw. It was just as crucial to maintain this demeanor when glancing at the banners and signs above their shops. I did not want to seem as though I was searching for any particular shop. When I told my father that I would get directions by asking passersby, he responded that the signs might help me as well. Every shop sign will have its name and the owner's name on it, he said to me as my mother, standing behind him, added her own commentary, saying that the signs would steer me only to their shops when I needed to be guided to others. She spoke as if her playful mood were furnishing her with a cleverness she didn't usually possess, an adroitness of the sort that allowed her to show a widening gulf between herself and my father: the more mischievous she appeared, the more decrepit he looked. He seemed to confirm it by growing quiet or brooding over what he'd heard, not ready to respond. He looked like an old man whose mind was slowed by age, weakened and defenseless, with little recourse against whatever went on around him.

The few men I saw in that first street were occupied with their own business, their gazes remote, and they paid no attention to my intrusion. They seemed to have filled their shops with only the provisions that the apartment dwellers would need. I knew that what I was out here seeking would be some distance away, since those who might need what would fulfill my need were so few and so widely scattered. I would not find a trace of it here in this first street, nor in the street that began where this one turned, to which my father had bade me go. It was so narrow and twisting that I could not tell how long it was. The establishments lining its sides differed not at all from what I had just left behind me. The shop owners here had added nothing to what the previous ones had on offer, again displaying only the foodstuffs apartment dwellers would want. The shops here set these goods out exactly as the shops back there had done. And the merchants here, too, were still getting their shops ready for an onrush of customers who had not yet descended from the apartment blocks. It was from this second street—or from a junction here—that my father would begin every one of his beginnings, describing the streets and byways I must follow next. The intersection . . . a bit more than halfway down the street, I thought I must have missed it, because I could not distinguish one intersection from another, could not see anything I knew would precede it or would tell me I had gone too far. But my father hadn't been able to give me any landmarks as his hands sketched routes in the air, his eyes closed all the while; the map of tangled roads he made for me had no fixed points.

From there, or from here; from these intersections coming one after another, I would have to rely on instinct. Then, entering one of these crossroads, I suddenly realized that my father had not been guiding me to what I was after. He could not guide me, after all, because he'd never had occasion to know where it was or to happen upon it. He had remembered the streets only for what they held that was his. Or perhaps he was directing me to a point that he knew would lead to places he did not know. The street off this one was narrow too; in fact, it was narrower than the street leading me to it. Walking along it, what dawned on me was that I had made no progress, for the merchandise sold here did not offer anything more than what I had seen back there. But I didn't retrace my steps to the head of the street so as to take a different way. I figured I would have to arrive at something. When I reached the end, I would be somewhere.

Yes, I had certainly come out early. Likely, they would not be making themselves into a crowd before I was at least halfway to where I was going. They were still in their apartments in these narrow, hemmed in, jammed-together buildings that faced each other at such close proximity. They were still in their apartments: indeed, as I was reaching the end of the street, bisected by another narrow street, I was guessing that there was something—there must be something—that hindered or delayed their descent. To stop my father's continuous, circular charting of the streets, I had told him I would get directions from the people here—just like that, I'd told him despite my certainty that (even if I did try getting directions) it would be useless. They would no doubt give me names of places I didn't know. It would not help me at all, since they would not (I knew) start me off from a particular street and give me directions from there. I had no reference point from which to be guided. They would begin waving their hands just as my father does, and exactly like him they would sketch maps in the air for the sake of divulging what they knew, for themselves and not for me.

From there, from this next narrow street where I stop briefly to see if I can make out which direction to go, I decide that I had better begin by marking mental signposts that will help me to memorize the return route. Soon I'll have been down many streets, and it won't be simple to return, traversing street after street and taking one intersection after another. Coming back will be especially difficult because they're sure to have formed a crowd by then, and this will be one way that I'll miss the signs I have memorized.

Nevertheless, I must keep going along these streets that will inevitably take me to what I'm seeking out here. When he began wandering the streets, some time after we had moved, my father had gotten to districts much farther away than this, for he had seen rows of shops where one sold goods that the next one did not. Or perhaps he followed different routes to those places he would describe to us when he came home. I might be taking the wrong streets and getting farther away rather than closer to the place I must reach. I can ask which general direction I'm going, at least. That man who has just finished sweeping out his shop will answer me, pointing in one single direction rather than directing me to a mass of intersecting and intertwining streets. Go that way, from there, he says to me, and so I retrace my steps, still searching for a place where the shops sell something other than the foodstuffs these apartment dwellers need. I must ask someone, before the residents all come down to the streets and crowd the way. Once they have clogged my route I'll have to constantly extricate my body from them. And after every step I'll find myself face to face with someone who stares at me at the same time I look at him, both of us trying to figure out who will make way for the other. Or the person I ask for help will point me in the same direction I'm already walking, extending his entire arm as if to make me understand that I am still far from my destination and many streets lie ahead that I must walk down before I'm there. Instead of asking now, I will go on walking until I feel I've found a place where I don't mind asking someone.

And then, too, if I spot a change in what the merchants are selling, I'll know I have begun to get somewhere on my own. I will feel that I've gotten close, or at least that I'm beginning to get close when I see, for example, a clothing store or a shop that sells bed linens or pots and pans. I will sense that I have gotten close when I reach a shop that's bigger than the others I've seen, and so I'll know that it's meant for customers coming from streets farther away. That will tell me that I'm close, or that I've begun to get close, and I'll also know that I'm about to reach broad streets—wider than these, at least. They will certainly lead to still other streets where the shops sell things to people who come great distances to buy them. I will arrive there. I must do so, if I just go on walking. There's really no need for me to ask anyone, since such long stretches as these must be leading somewhere. But I must hurry. I have to get across as many streets as I can before they all come down from their apartments. They will slow down my walking. With the street in front of me filled with them, I will no longer be able to look ahead as far as a distance of three or four shops, which allows me to stay at a remove from what I'm seeing, to keep myself apart. They'll advance and surround me, I'll be caught in their midst while I try to detach myself from the crowd they make as they stare at me, each from his own direction, and I won't be able to keep from being hemmed in by people who are far too close to my body.

XIV

As I TURNED ONTO THE sand track, I could see the unmistakable figure of my father at the window, waiting for me
to return. I knew he had doubted I would make it back; that
was why he had heaved his body upward, hoping to see me
more clearly, and had even leant heavily out the window.
When the mass of shadow at the window was suddenly gone,
as he hurried away to open the door, I was puzzled. Surely
his eyes had not allowed him to see me clearly from that distance at all. Perhaps, ever since I'd gone out in the morning,
he had gotten to his feet many times, in that way of his, and
had headed toward the door. As I began to climb the stairs I
sensed his presence above me, hesitating between the open
door and the balustrade, which was not a place where he
would stand for long. As I came in, he was standing facing the
doorway, like anyone who stands to welcome visitors coming
in. But he was confused and watchful: I could see that in his
eyes, which were dilated and still showed a bit of clarity at the
edges that the illness hadn't yet contaminated.

He knew—was it from my empty hands?—that I had
not been guided to what I had gone out to find. He should
have gone with me, he said, and he added that I mustn't let
it upset me, since no one finds his way the very first time, to

something that lies in a place he doesn't know. He steered me firmly to the table where my empty plate sat flanked by fork and knife, looking as though it had been arranged and rearranged, time and time again. Leaving me to sit down, he announced that the food was still warm. While waiting for me to arrive, he had carefully kept it warm, lighting the flame beneath it every few minutes. He brought the little casserole over to me and asked if there was something else I wanted that he could make for me now.

Sitting down very close to me, he asked whether I'd been walking all that time. Or had I found somewhere to sit and rest? Had I gotten hungry or thirsty? Had I spoken to anyone who was able to help me get where I wanted to go? I used my hunger and fatigue to excuse myself from answering his questions with anything more than a quick gesture or a nod, or at times a few terse words that didn't tell him anything or console him. His string of questions didn't manage to get me talking spontaneously of my own accord, as if I were remembering things without having to be prompted. As if I was the one who had launched into talking about something I had encountered on my excursion, he grew quiet, letting me understand that the floor was now all mine.

I didn't say anything that amounted to anything about my outing, or about how he had waited for me all alone at home after my mother had gone out for that same little pleasure jaunt that had pleased her so much the first time. When he told me this, I had an image of her sitting out there, in exactly the same spot where she and the woman had spent their first day out. Finishing my meal, I felt no eagerness to have a look out there. Weary, I thought it likely that I would see the two of them posed exactly as I imagined them, and that sight would hardly relax or reassure me.

Finally he stood up, recognizing that our lapse into silence would not be broken by either one of us. As he headed for the kitchen I could tell he was being careful not to appear annoyed or to suggest that this abrupt rise from the table had anything to do with my silence or my absorption in my food. He had nothing to do out there in the kitchen. Nothing to cook, nothing to pick up and bring out here. All he could do was stare out of the window toward the patch where the two women sat, and he would not even be able to see anything but blurry shapes. Anyway, he wouldn't need to remain there long, standing in front of the basin or looking out of the window. He would not linger more than the few moments he needed to relieve his discomfort or to believe that by now I might be ready for some conversation.

We can go out together tomorrow, if you like, he said to me. I had finished eating but I was still sitting at my place with my hands set apart on the table as if to show my readiness for his return. Tomorrow we'll go out together, he said to me, as he sat down at his place. He was announcing the decision he had arrived at on his own while tarrying in the kitchen. When he saw that this time my silence meant I was thinking over what he had just said, he began with the help of the tabletop to sketch out our route from its starting point. To make me a part of his planning session, every time his hand swerved off the road he was tracing he would begin asking me whether I had gotten as far as that. He ignored the empty, dirty plate in front of me; he sensed that getting up to take it to the kitchen might distract us and shatter the delicate atmosphere of our collaboration. But as he began to go further afield from the linear routes he had marked out, I told him that I could go out by myself tomorrow. He took this as a question I was asking him, though, one he could answer by confirming that it was better for me if the two of us were together.

I had no desire to view the pair of them out there, nor any inclination to sit on the balcony that looked down on them as my father now invited me to do. When I went instead to my room, leaving him on his own, I had the feeling he had wanted to tell me something significant that would require him to prepare me with some preliminary words. He went on sitting there in his place at the table and didn't look around as I went to my room where, he knew, I would close the door firmly. Getting to my feet like this, I must have appeared as though I was silencing him deliberately or—just as consciously—setting him down at the starting line of a new period of waiting that he did not know how to get across. He wanted to convey something to me, but before doing so he wanted us to sit together.

He wants us to sit and talk first, so that it will seem to us as if we've arrived together, through the words we exchange, at whatever it is that he wants to tell me.

I left him there sitting by himself at the table. I knew that moments later he would rise to shuffle to another corner of the house, but he would not stay put for long and would move on to yet another spot. We leave him all alone by himself, I thought—but it was as if I were saying it out loud to my mother, and an image of her face bearing a silly smile flashed in front of my eyes. In its happy simplicity my mother's face glowed with freshness, though I hadn't cracked my window open to see her sitting there with the other woman. They would present exactly the same picture they'd presented the time before, sitting one beside the other silently as they stared into the emptiness at whose farthest point they could not see the old city. I was so far from wanting to see them that

I didn't even take a single step toward the window. My feet were weary after all of the walking I'd done. Probably they were swollen and blistered inside my shoes; when I looked down I saw that the laces looked strained and half-shredded and ready to snap from being too tight across my swollen feet. Undoing them, bending over as I sat on the edge of the bed, I thought that my feet would inflate suddenly like any body part whose confinement has squeezed and shrunken it. I had no desire to go to the window where I would look out on the two of them. They would be by themselves out there, and beside them would sit the very same articles they had toted with them the first time. The enormous umbrella would be stuck into the ground just as before, but it would spread out too far above them to give them any shade. I would not look out the window over to where they must be sitting, but I would begin my nap by imagining the sound of the wind coming to them from below and dwindling as it reached them and settled there quietly. I could also help myself to sleep by imagining a fly droning loudly as it circled endlessly around their heads. Then my mother's smiling face, so close to me, which I find irritating; and the legs sticking straight out, bare and facing the old city; and then the fly again. The fly droning and sketching its route in an oval, once through the air and then a second time until it reels in my head, which enters the circle at a particular point and begins to follow the route marked out by the fly, circling in turns and turns, time after time after time after

This was not real sleep, and my father's cautious knock on the door roused me. I opened my door to find him standing there with his fingers balled up to knock again. As I stood waiting he said he'd been anxious lest I was asleep. He was going to wait at the door a little before going back to what-

105

ever spot in the house he'd been sitting in. It looked to me as though the few minutes he'd spent alone after I had risen from the table had weakened him and altered his appearance. As I stepped forward so that we would be walking together, he explained that he had come to ask me whether we were going to go out together tomorrow. That was his excuse for coming to speak to me when he knew I was tired and needed to sleep. Those last moments he had spent by himself had weakened him. As I walked next to him or behind him, giving myself up to his determination that we sit down together where he wanted us to sit, I thought he seemed ready to bow to my wishes in exchange for my sitting with him and not leaving him alone. That's how he began to behave as we reached the sitting room. He stood there and looked at me, waiting for me to give him an indication of whether he should keep walking to the balcony or whether we would sit here on the small sofas. It was his way of paying me back for my willingness to sit with him and the fact that I had gotten out of bed for his sake. On the balcony where we finally sat down he extended his arms and hands fully along the arms of the chair so that they seemed to express both compliance and rest. When I began moving my chair nearer to his, he simply turned a neutral, indifferent gaze on me as if he were starting a process of withdrawal from his surroundings that would release him from whatever went on around him. I knew that he wasn't waiting for me to speak, just as I knew that he wasn't thinking about anything in particular. All he wanted was to sit and feel himself emerging from that interval that had tired him out, much the way anyone would feel upon reaching a place of safety that would shield him from an expected punishment or a certain danger. When his silence lengthened I asked him — me this time, asking him — if he wanted anything that I could make for him. He did not want anything; there was only that neutral gaze, inquiring without anticipating anything, the look that earlier he had turned upon my chair.

Being left alone had weakened and altered him. Out there, some distance away from the end of the balcony, I imagined my mother sitting with the other woman in that same silent get-together, uninterrupted except for a short time when they would turn to eating what they had prepared and brought from home. There, on the sand over which they spread their mat, my mother's face would still hold a smile as she enjoyed her flush of well-being. I asked my father again if he wanted me to make him something, and he shifted his eyes to me as he had before, but this time his gaze was sluggish and drowsy. He looked as though that sense of safety was lulling him to sleep. I knew I had to go on sitting there next to him when he dropped off to sleep, for even as he napped he would remain alert to whether I was still there. Though his eyes would be tightly shut he would open them suddenly as if something had surprised him as he slept, and he would look in my direction. Our leaving him on his own so much had definitely weakened and fatigued him. When he opened his eyes in one of those moments of alertness I wouldn't say to him that it would be better for him to sleep in his room so that he could actually get some rest, even if I could make him understand that I was saying this for his own sake. I wouldn't tell him to go and sleep in his bed even though if I did tell him that, I would follow it by saying that tomorrow morning we would go out together after all. I will not say that to him. I will leave him to sleep here on his chair as I sit beside him and wait, even though I am so very tired.

XV

IT WAS SO EARLY WHEN we went out that as we walked the sand track I assumed that the merchants would not have even come to their shops yet. Knocking on my door with the tentative rap that I had been expecting, my father was standing there in his outdoor clothes, having dampened his thin hair and parted it just as I do mine. Indeed, in the long interval since he had gotten out of bed, he must have re-ironed his clothes and polished his heavy black shoes again, though they would be coated with dirt and dust as soon as he took his first steps onto the track. I had suspected that he would wake up very early. More likely he had not gone to sleep at all. As soon as we stepped over the threshold and were outside the building, readying ourselves determinedly for the long streets we would walk, it seemed as if all of a sudden he had regained his old manner of walking, which gave his short figure that look of strength peculiar to short and stocky bodies, and a youthfulness that made me wonder whether, once we reached the beginning of the paved street, he would roll up his shirtsleeves, stopping only when the folds reached halfway up his arms.

He had slept little that night, or perhaps not at all. Going out with me to steer me to the right place was the first occupation he'd had since stopping his activities all those years ago. He had to prepare for it as old men do when they feel they're about to take something new in hand. I didn't sleep well either, given how tired out I was. Indeed this fatigue of mine, which I thought would send me into a sound sleep, instead kept me awake through most of the night. In the little bursts of napping from which I would soon awaken with a start, instantly alert, my father's face would come to me, very near. He was looking at me but those watery eyes didn't really see me, and they seemed to smile out of a face that was weak and strained.

Or his silhouette would come to me as it was before we went to bed, arms straight out on the armrests of his chair, sinking into his nap with a swiftness that terrified me, for I couldn't help wondering if this onrush would stop before it paralyzed his face and killed him. I did not get the sleep I needed that night. My weariness was too heavy to banish just by lying down on my bed and closing my eyes. As we walked together side by side on the sand track, my fatigue sat on me heavily, drying up my throat and making my head heavy. My father's face, still so close to mine, had not lost the look it had had in my interrupted naps—until I would glance at him and see him next to me, real.

The merchants on either side of the street where we turned in from the sand track presented the same scenario as the day before. That they had longer to wait today before their customers would come down seemed to make no difference in their activities. These shops in close sequence, packed so tightly together at this end of the street, were ones my father knew. As we approached their proprietors my father greeted them with a wave of his hand, greeting upon greeting, to which they replied with their hands in the air as well.

For him this was the opening sacrament of this work he was performing: with it he was showing me that as long as I was with him I would enjoy circumstances different from those I faced when I was on my own. Or it may be that with these first steps of ours, he was intent on trying to make me remember what he had been like in the days when we would go together to his shop down in the old city. He greeted these men whose shops followed so closely upon one another; he greeted them in turn, giving the appearance that he was one of them and was intimately familiar with their work routines. It probably pleased him no end when the men paused in whatever they were doing to return his greetings, looking at us both all the while. These were something more than the usual glances, but my father couldn't see that they were looking at us for their own reasons — to satisfy their inquisitive nature and their curiosity — and not from something due to us.

Anyway, he stopped turning his face to the men in the shops after we turned off their street. In the long street where we now found ourselves, I had the feeling we had come into the area where I'd been yesterday, for here were the streets that stretched on and on so that we would do nothing but keep walking. Walking beside him, I had to quicken my pace to stay abreast, which made me appear to onlookers as though I were hopping or jumping across the ground, since my feet appeared to be my only moving parts. I didn't tell him to slow down, even when, to keep up with him, I had to go almost at a run. At the second intersection he turned to the left without any show of hesitation or uncertainty. And when he asked me, as we went down this street that went on and on in front of us, whether I had gone this way, his intent was simply to draw my attention to his lack of hesitation at the intersection; he had not slowed his pace for a moment. This was the same route I had walked yesterday. And I thought, as I hopped along beside him, that his coming with me had not added anything thus far to my own solitary venture. I had walked in these same streets without him, and indeed I had reached other streets. I wasn't sure he would reach them with the same ease.

No, up to this point he hadn't gotten me anywhere I wouldn't have gotten to on my own. In the street where a wide and straight road cut through, he had to look in both directions before settling on one of them. From the middle of the road, his weak vision didn't allow him to see signs or landmarks that might tell him where he was, so he had to choose a direction by relying on guesswork and instinct. To reassure me that we were taking the correct route, after we had left some buildings behind he gestured in one direction as if to anoint it as the right one. He reiterated this when, a bit farther on, his eyes encountered shapes he fancied he knew. That's the one, he said, reverting to his usual rapid pace that hesitation had slowed down. What could I do but follow him, especially since the streets I had been down yesterday had not gotten me to where I wanted to be? I remained silent when his hesitation became acute as new junctions appeared. Every time we reached an intersection, all he could do was rely on seeing something up close that might tell him where we were, for his eyesight could not get him any further than that. He couldn't see the street as he remembered it, since his eyes failed him in this regard. Once he was already walking down it he would go on looking to both sides of the street to convince himself, while he was walking, that this was the correct route.

But once here, he will not be capable of retracing his steps to that intersection he left behind, in order to begin again down another street. Or it will not happen with the simplicity he practiced when we were at home: losing himself in streets he remembered, he would return to a point where he could start off again in another direction. Out here, he wouldn't be able to correct whatever error he had fallen into by a mere wave of his hand, closing his eyes to remember where he'd been before taking the wrong turn and then returning there in his mind. Now, all the while he is walking, he must continually peer around, examining whatever he can see to make sure, with every new step, that this is the route he knows. This process slowed our pace. In the very long streets we would walk looking hard at everything around us just as if we were constantly facing intersections where we would have to choose which way to go. Aha, there it is, he would say to me, pointing to a shop he saw or waving at the façade of a building. Yes, this is it, he would say; but this certainty of his would soon fade as we went a distance in which he recognized nothing. This is what began to frighten him: the street we were in would fragment into uncertain possibilities. Either it was the right street, or it was the street we ought not to have taken. I have gone through here before . . . this street, I know it . . . he would begin saying after some moments of silence, having been gripped by a flurry of confusion during the time it took to walk by two or three buildings.

He could have asked the men who were in their shops, those that sold nothing more than the foodstuffs required by residents of these buildings, yet he would not do that unless he was very certain we had really lost our way. Did you go by here yesterday? he would ask, only to realize that he had not the slightest idea of how he would make use of my response. It would not help him at all if I were to answer, No, I didn't come by here. We had moved quite far away from the streets

I had learned yesterday, having turned off them to go down others. As we proceeded slowly among the people who had begun to come down from the higher floors of the buildings, the thought that came to me was that we were now in his streets, whether they were the right ones or not, for we were no longer in those closest streets of which we shared some knowledge. Read this sign, he began saying to me, wanting what I read to help him see something more clearly or to remember it. Read this, he would say, pointing to another sign or banner. It fatigued him to go on walking through the streets hesitant and confused. He was too tired now to see or to be able to read what he saw, even as close up as this. I knew that the only thing more walking would give him was further deterioration in his eyesight, and that it would not be long before he would be unable to see anything that was more than four or five steps ahead, barely enough for anyone trying to see where to put his feet and keep moving forward. Come on, let's ask someone, I would say, only to have him answer that I should wait a little, and in any case, the shop name I had just read to him had jogged his memory. But this didn't work out, either. It wasn't long before he came out of that space that was logged somewhere in his memory. They changed the streets, he began saying to me, going on to mutter something from which I gleaned only that the streets were no longer what they had been, and that they had spliced some new streets from the knots of old ones. When he meant for his words to be heard, he would turn directly to me to remark that they had expanded this new city of theirs, taking over more space, but that of course we would eventually reach areas he knew.

I had to wait for him to decide the moment when it became unavoidable: we would have to ask one of these people who were now so numerous around us, in and around the shops or walking in front of them or clustering in certain spots where they were doing nothing. But he couldn't do it. If he were to admit the necessity of asking, he thought, he would be acknowledging that it would have been better for me to come by myself and admitting that all he had done by coming with me was to usher me into these streets from which we didn't know how to get anywhere. Worse, this terrible failure would not just embarrass him but, to his way of thinking, it would mean that we would no longer listen to anything he said to us—to me and my mother—about anything. If we surrendered, he and I, and allowed passersby to show us our route, that would mean he was truly relinquishing the possibility of going out into the city, not because he no longer wanted to but because he no longer could. He knew the way, he said to me, and it was only his eyesight that had gotten him lost. He hadn't been able to tell the streets apart by sight even as his feet had gone into them of their own accord. What had made him get lost was his eyesight, he told me firmly. He was tired, breathing hard, and when I looked closely at his eyes I saw that they were empty and still, as if something inside wasn't working. At that point I didn't need to lose more time searching for someone to guide us. There were so many people around us, and all I had to do was turn my face a little to be directly facing someone whom I could ask. When I began talking to him my father stopped looking at what was around him and simply stood next to me, just like that, silent and looking at nothing.

XVI

EVER SINCE THAT EXPEDITION OF ours from which we returned tired and dispirited, my father had begun spending most of his time sitting on the balcony, even though out there he could no longer enjoy anything but the gusts of cool air coming from the deep emptiness below him. It had been a while now since he had begun to experience extreme eye fatigue and disease, and he could no longer see anything at any distance. The old city, remote and far below us, he could no longer see at all, for it was encased in the blackish fog that was now composed of everything his eyes could not distinguish clearly. He could see only nearby objects, and to do even that he had to bring them very close to his eyes if he wanted to see them as they really were. When he looks at me I assume that he sees me obscured and darkened, as if I'm covered by a dense and undulating smoky fog, just the way his eyes themselves seem covered. It's become hard to imagine their smooth surface beneath that nylon skin that has grown into the thick and wrinkled crust that covers them entirely.

Out there on the balcony, flush against the wall so that he can support his elbow on it, he no longer leaves the chair with its ottoman and back cushion that my mother sewed to allow him to sit a bit higher and straighter. He no longer enjoys anything but the surging puffs of cool breeze reaching him. He no longer asks what has happened to the shop in the old city that his finger, jabbing the air, was always seeking when we moved here. The whole of the old city has become a single façade now, a single direction to which he points with his hand or his head, making a single gesture that takes in all of it. Afterward he asks me where they are now. By this time, I know that what he means by his question is whether they have finished demolishing all of it. I tell him they have only a little work still to do, and he says to me that many things were left there whose owners should have taken them out along with their furnishings and goods. Or they should have made sure to be there during the demolition to extract these things from amongst the stones as the walls were taken down. He's remembering wardrobes and cupboards built to measure in the houses, and steel vaults in the shops of watchmakers and jewelers, which looked so solidly built and firmly attached that they seemed as if they had been constructed along with the walls themselves.

He enumerated many other things, among them the contents of the grand stores that did not have just a single owner who was always there along with his employees. They must have left all that marble where it was, he would say to me before adding that in the cinemas as well, they must have abandoned all those seats that were fixed in place, in rows. As for the curtains that had covered the screens, which consumed so much fabric that the cinema owners had to take them out to the enormous courtyards in order to even pleat them, they would have been left hanging. Sitting there, my father could not stop naming all the things that must be taken from the old city. One thing was always leading him to another, and when he remembered something else still, this seemed to make him happy, as if the thought of it had occurred to him at precisely the right moment. The electric meter boxes! he would shout to me, as if coming up with the answer to a riddle that had fatigued his brain. Doorbell buttons! he would say; they were all left at the entryways, by the doors. That was his game, his entertainment or solace; he was able to harmonize what he had already named with the new items, accommodating one thing to the next. He would grow genuinely sorry about what had been abandoned there. First, because of its cost and its worth, since nothing comes for free, as he would say; and then because, after all, these things were necessities of life, and everything that had been left behind must be bought again to replace what was lost.

That was his way, too, of expressing his fear that the funds he had remaining would dwindle to nothing. Or it was one of his ways. Another was his way of counting—every evening— the contents of the little chest and organizing the coins and bills into piles according to each one's worth. Every time my mother saw him sitting on his bed with the money spread all around him she would ask from behind the door why he was counting it again today, since we had not spent any of it since he last counted. She would raise her voice just enough so that he would hear it. No doubt she hoped that the suspicion would enter his mind that she went about describing him just this way when she talked about him to anyone else. He didn't answer her while the money was scattered over the bed. He waited until he had put it all back, organized by value and in rows, to say to her, as he returned the chest to its place in the wardrobe, that it was better than spending his time standing in front of the mirror.

When she stays silent, giving him no answer, I know what she is thinking but cannot say. All the mirror will show him if he stands in front of it is his ugliness. Instead she turns and walks away quickly, as if wanting to put some distance between her exit from the room and his going out after her. She needs nothing more than these few steps to regain her smile, which she displays, here on the balcony, with a playful and casual air. With that smile she gives the appearance of successfully leaving behind the aftermath of their spat, and now here she is once again as she was before, showing how distant she is from him, and how different. It's as if this heedless smile of hers puts him back in his place, or at least sets him again where he was before that little scuffle brought them together briefly. But she won't stop with this. She will stand on the balcony for only a short interval, as part of her preparation for going out. This is how she will augment the distance she began to create with her smile: to it she adds her punishing retribution. He falls for this immediately, looking around in confusion at her comings and goings between the kitchen and the bedroom mirror as she gets herself ready to go out. I assume that as he does this he believes that no one sees him; for as he jerks his head from side to side in response to her movements, he's showing his own submission to her authority and thereby enhancing her power.

Indeed he all but follows her as she walks toward the door, her gait as unsteady as always. He waits to hear the sound of it closing before he turns away and looks helplessly around him to figure out where he should go now, and then he heads for the chair anchored against the balcony railing. If he encounters me standing still in the sitting room or coming out of the kitchen to go to my room he tells me that she has gone, which only confirms his position and makes it easier for her to punish him. He does not like to see her leaving the house; knowing this perfectly well, she is careful to spin out her preparations so that his state of bewilderment in her busy presence is protracted and his response to the dilemma she puts him in all the more anguishing.

So she has gone, he says, staring at me as if this means I should do something. She will still be on the stairs. All we can hear is the heavy, muffled sound of her steps, as he turns away and adopts the demeanor of someone baffled by the fact that no one here can help him. He almost seems to believe, whenever she goes out, that she has gone out for the last time: that this is her final exit, that she will not return. He seems to think so even though he knows she is there, just below, and all her return requires is climbing one flight of stairs. While she's gone he remains in his chair. He doesn't try to get up even briefly, for he has come to know that even if we sit together, we will not talk. Likewise he has stopped asking me—every time he senses from where he sits that I'm going to the kitchen—whether there is anything I want.

He is there in his chair when she comes back. His hand grasps the railing as if he's readying himself to stand up, but then he brings his head forward in order to learn, without turning his head, where in the house she is now and what she is doing. She is in her bedroom right now, and not in the kitchen or the sitting room. There, where she leaves the door half closed behind her, she adds another interval to her spell of remoteness from us, by staying in that room where no one will pass by unless they are expressly going there.

He waits for her to be in the kitchen or the sitting room. But there, too, she maintains this spell of distance from us, since her heavy gait sounds wobbly, the same as when she left. She's still in her high-heeled sandals that compress and all but splay open to each side under her large, heavy body, or her heaviness drops into the heels, making them look as though they've sunk into the floor tiles like nails firmly lodged there. Her clothing is tight across her body, and this particular dress accentuates how large she is, how very prominent are the swellings under the tightly stretched fabric. Commenting on how my father hates seeing her standing in front of the mirror, she remarks to me that she's not costing us anything by doing this. He washes too, she says, as if to make me understand that with all her décor and finery she is using nothing more than a simple bar of soap, which is not even scented by anything other than its own basic fragrance and which, when she washes herself with it, gives her face a uniformly glacial hue. Women color their faces, she says to me, as if to make me understand that, alone of all women, she does not blanket her face with powder and tint.

She does not cost him anything by going out or by standing in front of the mirror. And her clothing, as stretched and worn as it is, will keep her close by, as much as she may have a penchant for making visits. She'll go no farther than the apartment beneath us or the spot where they sit outside, there on the sand, and where no one else will see her. These tight garments she can only substitute with dresses that are even tighter. In her bedroom she forces her large body into clothing that disfigures and dishonors it. That dress with the collar wings hanging down to her bosom on her will look like something a foreign woman would wear. The same goes for the navy blue dress made up to look like a sailor's togs.

Anyway, all the clothes in the wardrobe seem to have been tailored for a different body. She has grown so much fatter now that she can't even let out the seams in order to widen the dress, since these dresses were never made in the first place with any extra margin of fabric. And she doesn't like to refashion them—making a dress into a blouse or a

122

skirt—because the minute you put a pair of scissors to a dress, you ruin it.

Soon enough she'll return each dress to the wardrobe on its hanger, from which she didn't even remove it. All she does is take these dresses out and look at them, as if to simply make certain, yet again, that wearing this one or that one would not be suitable for the moment. Still, she returns them to the wardrobe exactly like old belongings whose time will come, she figures, and when it does, she can revive them. Anyway, no one throws away anything unless it can be replaced with something else. Besides, wardrobes that are made to hold clothes must remain full of clothes. Filling! says my mother about her old clothes that she has abandoned but also kept. They're filling for the wardrobe, she adds as she comes out of the room dressed in the same thing she had on when she went in. Tight and worn and faded, it does not restrain her heedless, playful smile, which appears a moment or two after she has emerged.

XVII

MORE THAN ONCE, HER HEAVY steps clattering against the floor tiles, she has intimated to me that she's going to their place, below. She gives me that sly and teasing look, which means that she knows what's what with me and that she's telling me I can, if I wish, go down there with her. As she's conveying this, I have the impression that she has transformed her irritation into a sport that is no less fevered or reckless. And with this wicked little intimation of hers, she is returning me to my little-boyhood, a lad absorbed in the suddenly suspect look on a familiar face, a cagey expression he has never seen on it before.

But after all, she did succeed in getting me to follow her in her excursions. The first time, I followed her out to where she would sit down—she and the woman—out there on the sand. I didn't wait until the two of them had already arrived at their spot. Someone standing at my window, just overhead, could have seen me walking behind the two of them, hurrying along, my feet flapping in the sand that pulled me downward as I tried to catch up. Despite all the things they were carrying that weighed them down, they arrived before I did. They didn't see me until after they had put all their various trappings on the ground. He has come, I heard the woman saying as she stared at me, as if her eyes couldn't detach themselves from my sudden appearance there, which had startled her. Then she put her hand out to me in greeting while I was still several steps away. That allowed me to slow down the usual jerk of my shoulder, a quick and wrenching motion that helps my hand to extend farther out or higher in the air.

My mother believed that it was the woman who kept me at my window; that she was the one who led me to spy and eavesdrop as I moved through the house. Out there on the sand, her face had a doubting expression as she put out her own hand, after the woman had done the same, to shake mine. It was as if, as soon as she saw me, her face bubbled over with that imbecilic joy of hers, but at the same time it showed the uncertainty of a schemer who knows there is much left to accomplish. When I saw that the woman was acting flustered and unsure of how to position herself on the mat they had set down, clearly wondering how the three of us would arrange ourselves, I figured that my mother must have made some progress already in furthering her plot, perhaps starting by telling the woman that I lurked there behind the window. As the two of them sat down, leaving an empty space on the mat where I could sit, I had the uneasy feeling that if I stayed I would see my mother in a position that would make me deeply uncomfortable. But here she was already insisting that I sit down. Come and sit down, come on, she began saying to me as her eyes took on a look of confusion about what she was preparing for and what she would do next if I really did sit down.

This time, too, my mother triumphed in getting me to follow her. When the woman opened the door to her home for us to come in, my mother seemed more sure of herself, preparing to shake hands with the woman and to initiate an exchange of greetings. Indeed, before we even reached their sitting room, which was directly below the room we used as a dining room, she was getting ready to launch her provocative little gestures that would add new meaning and significance to whatever she actually said, making her words more comprehensible. When the woman withdrew as if she had an urgent task, calling her to one of the other rooms, I sensed that she needed these few moments in there to rid herself of a nervousness she feared would show all too clearly. Their home was laid out differently than ours was. The salon and the adjoining room, which they had made their sitting room, were separated by an arch supported on two white marble pillars. The floor tiles had a different pattern and were older than ours, though they had a higher gloss. They looked to me as if they were made from a more pliant material that would feel softer to the bare feet that I instantly began to imagine sticking to them from sweat that had half-dried on them and gone tacky.

When the woman came back from wherever she had been, further inside, I was convinced that she hadn't done anything in there but soothe her nerves. She appeared calmer now, and to confirm it she began welcoming us again as she tugged her tight dress downward so as not to reveal her legs when she sat down on the little sofa opposite us. She began pulling on it again as soon as she was seated, and my mother said to her with another wink that she should sit however she liked and relax. I was uneasy and somewhat exasperated at my mother's winking. I thought it would return the woman to her state of agitation; only her question to my mother seemed to extract her from it: Why had my mother gone upstairs early yesterday? But in spite of the woman's apparent bashfulness and confusion, the two women appeared to me as though they had come to some sort of understanding about what my mother was attempting to do with her comments and her winks. And not so much through these hints and suggestions, which surely left each of them to act on her own, but rather with a pact they seemed to have made in which, no doubt, my mother had dictated each step and each bit of timing. So the woman had accepted me then. Faced with her confusion, I certainly had the sense that I could settle myself on the sofa in whatever position would be most comfortable for me, not worrying about holding my head rigidly high to prove that I had a neck above my chest. So she had accepted me, and my mother was thinking that she would have to do nothing more than verbally conduct us as far as necessary to get us to do what she expected us to do.

The sight of the woman's legs set me on edge. It was no use: every time I glanced at her, trying to keep my eyes level with the top of her head, I could still see them. Pressed together, their whiteness only appeared more emphatic, the skin stretching tautly across the mounds of her thighs so that the surfaces looked especially smooth and soft while emphasizing the fleshiness beneath the skin. The sight of them unnerved me, yes, and in my dread that my eyes might slip irrecoverably to fasten on them, I no longer found it enough to raise my eyes as far upward as I could, but rather, I began shifting my gaze from one end of the room to the other, staring now into the corners and now at the walls. When I looked at my mother she seemed to be closely observing what was playing out before her, the expression on her face a blend of dopiness and slyness. When she realized that we might well go on sitting here in this silence, she said to the woman, with another incautious wink, that she had not done anything yet to host us properly.

When the woman got up to go to her kitchen I almost asked my mother if there was anyone else in the apartment. From her room in there — and I knew exactly how far its door was from where I was sitting — I could hear not a single one of the sounds that I knew so well. But the way the woman sat across from us tugging at her tight dress told me that no one else was at home. They had contrived all of this, she and my mother. No doubt the two of them worked together to get the place ready and to arrange how the woman would remove her daughter. Even to the point that my mother, wanting to show that we could behave freely and however we wished, began to lean forward, lifting her massive backside as she batted the sofa cushions with her hand to fluff them up evenly before she returned them to their places. The two of them had made her leave the house and surely they had shut the door to her room as they busied themselves straightening and rearranging. Still, I did consider asking my mother if anyone was in the house but us. Not to hear her response, which would be nothing more than another series of hints and insinuations, but so that I could ask her then whether I could look over the apartment to see how it was divided up and how its rooms were situated. From the little sofa where she sat, my mother asked the woman in a loud voice if she needed help with anything. When the woman's voice came back after a moment's delay my mother got up and said that she was going in there. I knew that the two of them must have neglected some detail in their arrangements and they were meeting to rectify that. Alone in the sitting room I could look around at everything without feeling any embarrassment or confusion if they were to appear suddenly, since it wouldn't look as if I were spying or being overly curious. I would just be trying to entertain myself, that's all, trying to pass the time as I waited for them to return. High on the wall, which had no windows and doors to interrupt the space, hung a picture in a voluminous frame: men and women in flowing, old-fashioned dress were gathered, necks and heads craned, waiting to descend to a boat separated from the ledge where they stood by no more than the span of a step or two. The picture, on fabric, had not been done by hand. The work was too perfect for that, the colors too well matched. Below, though, the armrests and backs of the sofas were covered in pieces of finely worked, lacy fabric that was repeated on the surfaces of the cushions placed at the ends and midpoints of the sofas. As the sound of their low, staccato voices, which I could not make out clearly, reached me from the kitchen, I noted that the apartment's cupboards and shelves didn't hold anything that men wear or use for their personal needs. In their bathroom, too, there would be only the tools and powders that women use — the bathroom, whose location I also know, even though if its door were open in front of me now I would find it to be different from our bathroom, directly above it. Not only the color of the tiling on the floors and walls but also how the fittings and shelves are arranged. The bathroom, in which without a doubt certain things of hers have been left sitting out. Her small underclothes will be arranged neatly in the narrow cabinet, which is also in a different place in their bathroom than it is in ours. I might even find her panties, the ones she had taken off most recently, slipping them down over her legs; small and white, they would have been left in the corner next to the door. Or I would find the miniature towels, the kind shaped and worked like handkerchiefs, with which she would dry herself after every trip to the bathroom. Or I would find, on the edge of the basin, a razor blade still on the razor head, cleaned of the hair that had been plucked and shaved — light hair that has not yet coarsened. The bathroom, which I will not be able to enter on any excuse or pretext. For I would be going where the two of them, she and her mother, go only in a state of undress, intimate with their naked, private parts.

We kept you waiting, the woman said as she stood in front of me bending slightly forward, holding out a tray on which sat three glasses of iced orange blossom–flavored syrup. As she did so, she brought her face very close to mine. Moving my head back slightly, I understood that she did this with my mother's encouragement. It seemed as if I were their guest, the two of them together, for both women remained standing in front of me as each one took her glass from the tray without any of the ceremony normally accorded guests. When they sat down, maintaining their silence, I realized that they had agreed on something and each was waiting for the other to begin. But the woman, who set her glass down on the table next to her, went on pressing her legs together and pulling her tight dress forward to cover her knees. My mother asked whether anyone wanted anything from the kitchen before getting up from the sofa, her nearly empty glass in her grip. Stepping between us, she turned toward the woman and leaned down to pick up the tray and the woman's nearly untouched glass. Then I could hear the water gushing from the tap and I knew she would stay in there, occupying herself by slowly washing the glasses and then looking out of the big kitchen window, leaving us alone to do the thing she was waiting for us to do, or at least to begin doing it. As soon as she could see that we had begun to talk, she would say that we'd left my father alone and she was going up to him.

131

XVIII

In my room, leaning out over the window ledge, I can bring her bare shoulder so near to me that I can practically feel it with my eyes. Her real shoulder, I mean, and I can actually feel myself touching it. I'm imagining this, and it's being interrupted now and then by an abrupt, loud movement she makes. She has lost something that she doesn't want anyone else to find before she can locate it. She jumps up from the edge of the bed where she sits facing the wardrobe and staring at its closed double-panel doors, going over to it several times. Or she might stand there on the edge of the bed, stretching herself as high as she can to peer over the top of the wardrobe, to see if what she's missing is there. There below me, she is (I know) completely caught up in her frantic, solitary search. She won't think about the fact that her mother can hear the sound of drawers being slammed shut, one after another, after she has turned her carefully organized belongings upside down. She won't know about me, or she won't care if she does have any sense that I'm lingering here above her, concentrating my ears and dangling my head in her direction. Even if she were to catch sight of my shadow hunched in the little corner of light out there on the square of sand, she will not be quick to realize that a body sits crouched just above her. When she came into her room that first time, in haste and irritation, I got up from the pages I was reading, still carrying my pen in my hand. I was certain that she would not have come back into the room only to leave it again immediately. Or if she did go out, I thought, she would soon come back, as much in a hurry and just as exasperated.

I was certain of this from the moment she first came in. So hearing her pushing open the door with both hands wasn't enough to tear me away from the papers I was reading. I had just been thinking about what she would look like as an image imprinted on that mirror in her home, that pale mirror framed in gilt. What I had seen in that moment as I was leaving their apartment with my mother was simply my own image of her, in an empty home that she moved through naked. In the mirror, her hair was loose and she covered her chest with it, though the nipples showed through, small and dark red. All I needed was the mirror in order to see her standing naked in it. And while my mother was talking to the woman, who opened only one panel of the double doors for us, I stole little glances at the mirror as if trying to make out something I wasn't supposed to see, or as if they—the woman and my mother—would know what I was looking for and why, and so I had to be careful in case they caught me staring. I was sneaking every look at the mirror that I could get. While in their home, I had only been able to look at my immediate surroundings, and as I followed my mother out the door, I began to suspect that this had been part of her plan as well. She did not want me to see anything but the woman sitting opposite me. As she mounted the stairs, she was tense and angry, as if by getting up when she did, I had thwarted the plan she had sketched out. I will come back, she said to me as she got up from her seat. Wait for me, I'll come back, she said again, gambling with a sudden recourse to direct and even bossy speech after all her play with insinuations. But I rose to my feet, with the excuse that I had a lot of pages upstairs that I must finish reading right away.

In the room below me, she has even lifted the mattress from her bedstead to see if the thing she was looking for was there. When she let a corner of the heavy mattress drop I could hear it clearly, and right after that she kicked something with her foot and I heard a shriek of objection and pain. Several times she opened the wardrobe doors and yanked the drawers out, shoving them loudly back after rummaging through the jumbled belongings inside. When she didn't find what she was searching for this time either, she went out again, propelled by her anger, to snap at her mother, who had left her on her own to search for whatever it was she had lost.

She will not remain out there away from her room for more than a short spell, during which I can lower myself from the window ledge to look at the papers I left on the table or go into the kitchen to get some water. But I hurry to return to my post leaning on the window frame. Or at least I'll stand next to the window waiting to hear the sound of her arrival rising from below. Nothing must elude me; nothing can happen unless I know about it from the start. Just as if I am monitoring a discussion that will get away from me if I'm at all late getting there.

I have to remain there, supporting myself on the windowsill or standing very close to the window. That way I will hear her not only as she enters her room, but also in the hallway as she approaches it. Or I will hear loud but unintelligible sounds coming from in there where her mother sits. But that won't last long either, since she will quickly return to her room and slam the door once she's inside. Hearing that, I can see her. And it's as if she has suddenly matured even more; her anger and exasperation, I imagine, have grown beyond the fury of a child.

At the window, as I work to hoist my body up and across the sill, I'm struck by the certainty that I must work quickly, even if I'm not sure what hurrying would mean and what it is I must do. All I know is that I must hurry before any more time passes in which the force of her anger—springing from the same root that yielded her body's yearning, captured as she stood naked in front of the mirror—catapults her out of her childhood and into an abrupt adulthood. This hungry desire teaches her the hows and whys of her body. It instructs her, too, as to what she should do were I to rest my hand against her neck or catch hold of her foot on some sort of pretext, wrapping it in the palms of my hands. She will give me a look meant to scold and threaten. It is that very look of terrible vexation that I imagine on her face when she comes back from in there, bumping hard into the door panel as she comes in and then slamming the door behind her.

I must hurry: I must get there before she grows up. Balancing my body with my stomach pressed onto the windowsill, which lifts my feet up off the floor, I think about the fact that what is maturing her into adulthood are these emotional flare-ups, which are far more tempestuous than the childish outbursts to which she had been accustomed. I also think about how, if I could somehow be near to her from now on, I'll have to figure out in advance what course to take and what excuse to offer, before reaching my hand out to her. Her body is no longer ignorant of its desires. If I were to touch her in places, I would no longer be drawing out a first longing from a body that had not yet known desire. I will not be able to touch her or take hold of her foot, or tease her, all the while claiming that I am doing nothing. So I must hurry. I must truly hurry. On the stairs, my mother was tense and angry; she did not turn to look at me, or say anything. When we reached our door she turned her key in the lock and marched in without making way or waiting for me. She left me standing at the door as if, by pretending to ignore me, she was leaving to me the choice of whether to come in or to do the other thing. Once she was inside our apartment, her anger did not fade as she whipped from room to room. Her head held high and her bosom rigid, she seemed to be punishing me for spoiling her schemes. Or—and this is what I hoped would happen—she was using her irritation to get ready for the next round, when I must not disappoint her as I did the first time.

I have to hurry. I must, and I know I won't need to say anything to my mother, because she'll take it upon herself to make all the arrangements for another visit downstairs. Tomorrow perhaps, or the day after, she'll look at me as she is leaving. She'll give me that insinuating look that invites me to follow her. Or she will speak, confronting me with the question I must answer: Do you want to go down? That's exactly what she'll do, as if holding out the bait to me and then binding me to act according to whatever answer I give her.

Yes, she is in her room now, just below me. She stands in the middle of it, surrounded by wardrobe doors flung open and drawers pulled out to tip precariously from their slots. She is in the middle of the room, precisely at its center. She has not found that thing she lost, but the efforts she has expended in looking have tired her and dissipated her anger. From where I am, propped up on the sill and hanging over it, I can come even closer to her reddened face, her hairline dampened by sweat. She is in the center of the room now, turning her wilted gaze on what lies around her. In a few moments her weariness will overcome her, when submitting to the loss of that object adds to her fatigue, and instead of remaining standing as she is now, she'll retreat to her bed to sit on the edge of it, turning her eyes in the same directions over and over but with less interest now. I must hurry. As the two women prepare to have me come down, they will banish her from the house. But they will not be able to keep her away every time. I must be quick. Soon my mother will forget this disappointment of hers. She'll resort to her usual winks and hints as she heads down to their place. Or she will open the door to my room to say to me, winking also, that she is going *down there*. But I will go down without warning, without the two of them having prepared for it by removing her from the apartment.

She remains in her room, sitting on the edge of the bed, absorbed in examining a little spear of dried skin that has separated from the skin around a fingernail. Or she is looking just as closely at her palm, all of it, and turning it over to look at the back of her hand. This is the aftermath of her revolt, which no doubt has ripened something in her body by sending the blood running faster through her veins. It's as if, sitting there on the edge of the bed, she's resting after it has come to a close, or simply after its eruption. She is in the state of calmness that she needs. She'll go on like this, engrossed in something intimate and giving herself some rest by examining whatever it is that occupies her, until, when she does get to her feet, it will be as if her movements are guided by meek and submissive hands. For I can tell that she has gotten up now; I can hear it. Here she is, taking her first step away from the bed. She's yawning, stretching her body upward and raising her arms overhead, reviving herself and enjoying the fatigue in her body. Then she takes the next step, which puts an end to her body's yawns and shudders. That second step forward takes her toward the window and not to the wardrobe where the doors and drawers are still open. She is coming toward the window; she has moved beyond the middle of the room, which means her shadow is beginning to come forward too, into the square of light that sails out aslant from her room. She is coming forward to meet my shadow that sits in the corner of the lit-up patch, or at its very edge. She has reached the window and now here she is leaning against it on her arms, which I can see beneath me. I can also see her light, golden hair, hanging thickly from her shoulders, which I can also glimpse, close to me and exactly as I have imagined them. My shadow has not left its place, there at the corner of the light or at the line its edge makes. And it will stay there, where it has fallen, hunched and motionless. She'll see it or rather will see something in it, if she applies her mind to what her eyes are seeing. She will see and recognize it from seeing her own shadow first, how it covers a certain area in the square of light. It is her shadow, out there, and this will alert her to the other shadow that lies above it, hunched and absolutely still.

She has dangled her arms over the windowsill to give them some rest and to idly balance her body at the same time. That has lifted her higher, tugging her nightgown up from the middle. From my niche I can see her body from the back, swaddled and stretched taut. She has not seen my shadow yet. She goes on dangling like that as if she's amusing herself by getting as near as she can to the sand below. She pays no attention to my shadow, or doesn't recognize it for what it is, until she brings her arms upward and stretches her body as if she wants to lift it off the windowsill.

She saw it then, and she knew what it was. It surprised

her into looking around suddenly, first at the area surrounding the building and then at its wall. In order to see me above, she would have to not only bend her head and shoulders back but twist her entire body around as well. I was still there, gazing at her below me, calm and relaxed, just as if I wanted to make her understand that if I am standing here right now, I have been standing here for a long time.

XIX

THE PAGES THAT SIT ON the table facing a similar pile of papers are what I turn to once I have closed the door. Line for line they are identical: I read a line over here and then reread it over there, simply to verify whether I read exactly the same words on each. This is the sole harvest of my wanderings through the web of streets, the only thing to which I was led in the end: the place where I was given nothing more than two sets of identical pages. This is what my father calls work; moreover, to his way of thinking it is agreeable, restful work because I do not need to leave the house every morning, as other people do who work. I could almost say the same about it, since whenever I feel like going to my room I can say that I have work to do. I read a line from over here and then the same line over there on the page that is supposed to be identical. This is what it has come to, all my reading in these books which, every time I added another one to the lot, I thought was expanding something inside of me. These leather-bound books with their old paper with its distinctive smell: as I read them I imagined myself rising from them afterwards with a new aspect, an image I wanted for my own. But these books of mine have brought me to nothing more than staring at two identical pages that I turn over on the table together so I can begin staring at the pair that follows them, from the top of the page, from the first line.

Every time I get to my feet to go off to my room, I say I have something I must finish. Lifting himself slightly from his chair out of respect for what I will do in there, my father begins wishing me good health and vigor: that's what he says, just as if I am now at the pinnacle of success. As for my mother, she hardly calls this work. She echoes the number I mention, seeming to say that what I earn is too little to place me in the category of a man who works. She seems to mock me as I rise to go to my room when she thinks I'm going in to read and compare my pages. Sometimes she launches into questions about what they do with the pages after I've read them, suggesting that she thinks perhaps they throw them away because they're worth so little, or at best they ignore them. I have also come to believe that perhaps they don't need them for any real task or project. Or I've begun to think that I am not doing anything that would merit even the pittance I earn. I think this because each time I carry these piles of paper back to them I perceive that I've put in a lot of work but I have done very little.

Or, when she sees me coming out of my room, my mother asks me how much I have worked. What she means is: What could one buy with what I have earned from my long session of reading? Even without her questions I find myself doing the same thing, comparing my hours sitting in front of the pages with the amount of food they would buy and how much of our needs that would satisfy. And I find that my father, sitting alone time after time with his little money box, counts and carefully rearranges a mound of coins that continues to dwindle despite my work. Nevertheless, he gets up from his chair for me whenever I say I'm going to my room.

Maybe he thinks this is only the first phase of my work, and I will advance beyond it.

He rises from his seat for me and then sits back and watches me going. When I'm getting ready to go out—having finished whatever pages are in my possession—he accompanies me, standing in wait at doors and in hallways as I move through the apartment. As I descend the stairs I know he is still standing there, as he was when he said goodbye to me; I know he won't shut the door until he calculates from the sound of my footsteps that I have reached the front entryway below. And still I haven't left his listening ears behind, even when I'm outside and beginning to walk along the sand track. Leaving the front entrance behind me, I set out with determination, with the fabric satchel—which my mother pulled from our belongings so I could drop the pages into them—hanging from my shoulder. This means *she* will not see what I am carrying if she stands at a window in one of their rooms looking out across the sand track. Her mother will not see what I carry either, though no doubt she is aware of my departure and may be standing at her window so that she can see me without my mother standing over her to egg her on. I make this journey every ten or fifteen days in order to return their papers to them and bring back new ones. The books I used to read have not brought me to anything greater than this. Those books I lived between, or among; those books that were my life, books that are never the same as they were when we saw them in a bookshop or in the workshops where they make them. Each time I arrive there and begin to mount the narrow steps that are hemmed in by walls so close together that one wall almost folds into the other, I decide that they must have hidden themselves away like this deliberately. They haven't hung out a sign to tell people that they are there, up above; and, since they don't know their neighbors and their neighbors don't know them, they've made it impossible for anyone to ask in these streets about their whereabouts. They're up there at the end of the narrowest and steepest stairway, which I think (every time I climb it) can't lead anywhere except to their entrance, with no threshold separating it from the stairs that are covered with the same tiles. When I get there I'll need to rest, not from the long route I followed but from the stairs, where I find myself pressing my hands to the walls as if to keep them back, or even to put more space between them so they won't come any nearer to me, imprisoning me when the space is no longer wide enough for my body to pass through. I will have to rest, there on the metal chair they've placed in the corner of the outer room, setting down the cloth bag whose strap must have made an obvious dent in my shoulder by now. This is one of those cheaply and quickly erected buildings where the upper floors are constructed of flimsy building material. My father preferred sitting at home to renting a shop in one of these buildings. They are putting their shops under the stairs or in the entryways of buildings, he would say to my mother, passing on to her—and to me—what he had seen in his wanderings through the streets. I am now on the uppermost floor of just such a building, waiting for someone to come out of the inner room so I can ask him whether I should go in. There, in front of a desk whose expanse doesn't suit this cramped and tiny room, I won't stay long. I won't stay any longer than the time the person sitting there needs to select a few pages from the pile and leaf through them to see whether I really did what I was supposed to do. I don't remain in that inner room for very long, only for the moments he takes to riffle through the pages, and in the end to give me another two sets of pages that I put into my "briefcase," which is really nothing but a black canvas bag. As for my wages, I have to wait for them, sitting there on the same metal chair, waiting and waiting while I know they are engrossed in figuring out the sum and counting the money. I assume that what delays them is their regret at being forced to pay it.

It doesn't amount to more than a few tattered paper bills, which I fold in half and put carefully, before leaving, in my pocket. On the way back my hand keeps dipping into my pocket to finger them every time I cross a street or switch the bag to my other shoulder. This is the only route I know, since nothing remains in my head of the circuitous paths that eventually led me to their office on the top floor, a single route I follow without glancing at the streets that branch off. These excursions with the black bag hanging heavily on my shoulder don't increase my knowledge of what might be there in those side streets that I do not walk. It seems that every time I walk this street and this route I distance myself a little more from any need to know any others. Nothing is left in my head of the streets I turned into back then, streets I went into and then retraced after reaching the ends or sometimes just going halfway down, streets of different lengths, some split by intersections, streets scattered here and there along my route. There is only one street, one route, that I need, a single street that seems to me like the only one I can possibly walk, or as though behind the façades of buildings on both sides the ground slopes downward to nothing, dropping further than I can see. Nothing lies behind the shops and building façades to each side. There lies my way which—every time I am again walking it—feels as though I cut its path myself, and now I'm penetrating and laying it open again, so that every time I traverse it I'm like a train car moving along the one and only set of rails that it knows.

I slice through the same road on my return, my pocket harboring the thin wad of folded paper bills. Once at home, I will watch my mother wince at how meager that wad is. As she sees me give the bills, still folded, to my father, she'll wonder out loud about whether I might shift to another sort of work or find another employer. I will be tired from all of the walking I've done and also from carrying my burden, which I will have set down; so I won't answer her, to tell her that I do not know how to work at anything else. Just the thought of searching for another office from which to bring sets of identical papers to read multiplies my fatigue and irritation. Once again I would have to loop through unfamiliar streets until I might happen upon another route that I would find uniquely comfortable among the city's new streets. I'm tired and I want to hurry into my room and change my clothes, which have grown heavy on my body, soiled by my long journey. The food is on the table, my father says to me. His eyes are open as wide as can be, as if he is gawking at an accident that has stunned him and he does not know how to react. The food is on the table, he says to me, but he doesn't beckon me there; his hand remains still. Nor does he encourage me toward the table by starting toward it himself. The bills are still in his hand, still folded, and he'll wait until he is alone, in his room with his money box, to begin staring at them as if he's reading them. He will set them carefully in the chest, arranged according to their denomination, and then he'll brush his hands together after returning the precious box to its place in the wardrobe. The food is on the table, he says to me when he returns and finds me changed into clothes I'm comfortable in. Now he does lead me by walking there himself, and once at the table he tests the warmth of the small casserole gingerly with his hand, as if he's put himself back into a state of bewilderment that makes his eyes widen. It's cool enough for my mother to handle; she takes the pan by its rim, with one hand, and carries it into the kitchen.

When she returns with it, now hot—she holds it with two hands this time—I think she's disdainful of the simple task she's done. She plunks the dish down carelessly on the table. She waits for my father to do what she hasn't done. He takes the lid off the pan, and steam rises from the food. Shall I serve you? he asks me. Or he might simply bring the pan closer to me, with both of his hands. She has gone back to her room or to the kitchen to return something to its place. She will stay away like this, unconcerned about how tired I am from walking so many long stretches in town. She is still not here when I finish eating and get up to go to my room to rest. It might be that she's allowing me the time I need to forget—myself—how tired I've become and how I must take that into account. As if she's giving me the time I need—or giving herself the time she needs—before once again, as she readies herself to go downstairs, to where they live, she can feel that her little signal to me might work as well as it did before. She'll give me the same studied but offhand glance that she follows immediately with a little nod of her head, slight but quick, as if she's asking me whether I'm ready to go down there. What she's asking is whether I am truly ready, or will I forsake her as I did before. Her careless little glance has taken on a kind of desperate offhandedness. She is trying to tell me that something between us has not changed. How she treated me would not change just because I was engaged in my work, which meant I left the house. Perhaps the minuscule amount of money I earn doesn't even deserve so many hours spent outside the house. And neither does it qualify me as the man who works inside this house, where the only role she knows how to play is that of a heedless and indifferent inhabitant, a woman who knows only how to play.

XX

WHEN WE WENT IN TOGETHER, though each alone, to her room whose door had remained closed, I did not yet know the woman's body. What I mean is that I had not looked at it sufficiently yet; all I had retained was the hue of her skin stretched over the flesh of her legs, and certain contours and curves that I could see when she had her back to me. We stood together in the room that the woman had darkened by closing the wooden shutters and lowering the curtains over them. Still, I could see her in the meager light that remained, just as she could see me, waiting as she was for us to begin that thing for which I imagine that she, like me, had made no preparation. On the dressing table with its expanse of mirror, which stood next to her, I could see little bottles of perfume lined up and looking as if they hadn't been moved for a very long time. The bed was neatly made up, and its broad surface somehow gave the appearance that it had looked exactly like this through all the years she had lived.

She looked confused standing there, placing her hand awkwardly on the table next to her, not knowing what else to do with it. I remained standing just inside the closed door; and from there, I sensed that she was more confused than I was. Perhaps she was expecting me to make the first move. I

149

could barely keep an abashed smile from curving my lips as it occurred to me that we were helpless without my mother. But that thought was quickly followed by the realization that in days past she had not been hinting to me alone: she must have been goading the woman, as she had me. She really ought to be with us, I thought, here in the room. She ought to stay close, with us, until we're in a state where we no longer need her.

But the woman took on the burden of making the first step, moving away from the mirror and going over to the bed, where she sat perched on the edge. Looking over at me from there, her gaze seemed feeble and tired and afraid of what we might do in the closed room. I didn't need to speculate much to know that my mother—who had gone up to our apartment on the pretext that she had work to do there—had come back. To be here, primarily, but also to safeguard the place from the possibility that the girl might return unexpectedly. When the woman gave me that long look from where she sat on the edge of her bed, it was as if she was imploring that we finish that thing we were to do, not begin it. I had to take the next step: to approach the bed, coming close enough that one of us would inevitably touch the other, a hand dropping and brushing against the other body. I was the one to do it. I took hold of her black hair, which was cut just shorter than shoulder length, and drew her head toward my face as I kept my gaze on her.

She staggered and nearly fell back onto the bed, but she righted herself, standing up to face me. When she turned away slightly and a little after that, lifted her arms behind her head, I did not know whether I should help her by undoing the fastener at the back of her dress. I didn't know whether I ought to go on looking at her as she unzipped it, her body opening out beneath it, where I could see how her bra straps had engraved deep lines from which the flesh bulged on either side. But as she fluttered her hands and then stretched them around behind her to lift her dress over her head, I jerked my face the other way, as if I didn't want to seem to be stealing furtive looks at what was being revealed in front of me. She took a step back, and it occurred to me that I should follow her example, beginning with my shirt, turning away so that she couldn't see me as I did what I was doing. After my shirt there was still my other shirt, the white cotton undershirt which, as I stood there holding onto it because I didn't know where to put it, seemed to me as shameful as it was shaming, leaving my body naked now, fully revealed.

As for her, although I was turned the other way I could tell that she had finished taking off her clothes and had lain down on the bed, covering herself with the sheet. She was waiting for me there. I didn't know whether her eyes were turned my way. The picture I had in my mind of my own body was of a sickly white mass that had never been exposed to view, and as for my large belly, whose roundness began high on my chest, I felt that I should avoid revealing it. Lowering my trousers, I saw the error I'd fallen into by taking off my shirt too far from the bed, but it didn't annoy me too much, since I could go on gripping a bit of my clothing, concealing my belly with it and not letting go of anything until I was there, like her, under the bedcovers.

When I turned to walk toward the other side of the bed, the empty side, I saw that she had brought the comforter up to her chin so that it covered her entire body. She wasn't looking in my direction. It was as if she wanted to stay hidden there, under the thick white duvet, her face visible only so she could keep her eyes open as if on guard, stationed over her concealed body. Seeing her tug the heavy bedcovers as high as she could, I recognized that it was best for me to do the same. I lay down on the empty half of the bed, keeping only my head uncovered. The sheet on the bed, like the fabric of the duvet, felt cold to the touch, and as I inserted my body between the layers of fabric I felt that now I had truly begun what I had come to do. Never before had I slept on a bed that was not mine; the smell of the fabric—the cocoon I had dropped myself into—seemed familiar. But it was an intimacy that belonged to others.

I could not go on lying there motionless, my eyes staring straight up at the ceiling, which separated this room from my mother's room. I would not stay in this position trying to imagine where and how to begin. The woman lying next to me, I thought, with the comforter held taut beneath her arms to hide her body beneath it, ought not to be so timid and embarrassed, since she must have done this many times. Wasn't it up to her to do something, to begin somehow? As for me, whatever I did first, I figured I need not do it with my hand. No, my small and not very powerful hand would not be what I would start with. If I raised it to her cheek first, or perhaps to her lips, it would be like exhibiting it to her. She would really see it as it is, small and incomplete and feeble. Or its smallness would be accented if I steered it toward a place that seemed to match it in size, her nipple for instance, which I had not yet seen.

She was completely naked beneath the comforter. I did not yet know her body, I thought. All I had preserved in my memory was the delicate skin across her legs, its fine, soft white hue captured by the light layer of fat beneath. I had not come to know her body yet. Before beginning I must expose it, look at it—all of it, lying flat and then standing upright, front and back, and from both sides. I would have to do that for the sake of distancing the woman slightly, pushing her far enough away from that image of her sitting with my mother or talking to her as the two of them sat together in their clothes that looked so similar on their bodies. But first I must do something to begin: let it be something beneath the comforter. My feet did not suffer from smallness or swelling. My legs were extended straight; now I raised my feet and brought them to the delicate pale skin that I did know, that white glow that rose from the soft fat collected beneath. I moved my foot and touched her skin, rubbing against it from high to low, and then repeated it in a single stroke that massaged the lower legs together. This is what I knew of her body. I knew what my feet were touching when they moved across the surface of her legs, held tightly together, and then up the sides of them. When she closed her eyes I withdrew my hand from beneath the covers so she would sense what I was about to do. I raised the comforter off her body. First to appear was her belly, white and slack and rounded as it sloped to either side. And then her chest: released from their prison, her breasts had spilled to either side; the circle of the nipple nearest me was broad and dark, protruding lightly from the flesh beneath. I did not need to start with my hand, cupping the nipple and what lay beneath. She might think that if this hand was tiny, then so was everything else about me. I need not start with my hand. It was no longer enough to bring my body close to her and press against her; I must turn toward her now as well. And then I would lift myself over her, beginning by kissing her, there on her mouth and around her mouth.

But while I was getting myself ready to actually do these things she turned toward me and put her hand on my body, just below my belly. And now she pressed her palm into me while bringing it close to the heart of the matter: to the core of what we would do. She closed her eyes, not from embarrassment at what she was doing but for the sake of capturing what she was about to feel, bringing it inside herself and keeping it there.

We were naked on the bed, visible to anyone who might be peeping through some tiny hole or spying from a place we couldn't see. The heavy coverlet beneath which we had concealed ourselves was now jumbled into a heap and sliding down to the bottom of the bed where my feet were. We were naked and visible to anyone who might spy on us. I didn't need to verify the presence of my mother, waiting in the sitting room, perhaps moving among its chairs. She was there; perhaps she would get to her feet every few minutes to stand behind our closed door trying hard to listen. Before I lifted myself off my side of the bed to get atop the woman next to me I must see her body, all of it, from there, where her legs are splayed wide apart as if waiting, or as if making space for that thing that will come forth from here where I am, at her feet, passing upward between her thighs to reach their furthermost, innermost point. I wasn't much preoccupied or bothered that the spying eyes were likely to be in place, staring. What those eyes would see was exactly what they would be imagining anyway, and what they already knew. The woman still had her eyes closed, and it looked as though whatever she was doing or receiving, she was sending straight to her dreams or somewhere inside herself, to hold it there. She gave no appearance of wanting to change position, stretched full length and spreading her legs, leaving only her hands free to touch me. When I put my hand out to the margin of her body and then to its center, doing the same thing, she let out a series of little sighs that I could see as much as hear, as though they were emerging from her absence itself, slightly rough and dry, completely unrelated to her voice.

She no longer flexed or moved her body, having turned toward me and then flipped over onto her back. It was as if, having spread her legs apart, she needed to do no more; she was offering what lay at the very end, that uppermost place that she had opened even as she seemed to guard it inside of her, while I remained at the outer limit. In this position, which she apparently wished to be her final one, and which she would not alter, I would not be able to make her curve toward me or to make any part of her move. I could not do anything but climb on top of her, advancing upward from her open legs. When I raised myself to her, my hands gripping what encircled the part of her she had opened, it seemed the only effect was to make her more rigid, more distracted with whatever was going on inside of her. Only her one hand that had reached for me remained against my body, clutching me. And when her hand came back to my sex, it seemed she would keep a firm grip on it, too, keeping me from moving closer to her, halting me where I crouched above her. Like the little groans she let escape that were so unlike her usual voice, the grip she held on me seemed to have issued from some obstinate fantasy in her head that became concentrated into a single, fixed and unchangeable image. Taking hold of me that way, and not budging from her own stiff position, she seemed to want to arrest my motions, keeping me frozen, hunched above her in a kneeling position with my hands clutching at what surrounded her sex. I even thought that the most she must want was exactly this; she would reach the summit of her pleasure that she could only find deep inside, on her own. To extract myself from this predicament she had created, and wanted, I had to enter her open sex. To touch the rim of it, first, with my tiny hand; and I wondered whether, in her state of absence—or trance—she would sense it as small, or sense it not at all, as it came into her, the size of a small child's hand. I didn't know whether she might be conjuring images in her head of what she felt, as if she were actually watching my hand rather than simply feeling it—perhaps— as it moved, hardly any bigger than her open sex. When I began to move my hand as if I was seeking out my path, I knew that I was beginning to awaken something inside of her, something happening in that closed space inside. She let out more sounds and gripped my sex hard. When she moved her legs further apart, opening her eyes a little as she did so, I understood that she wanted me to be right on top of her now and penetrate her. Indeed, the way she tightened her grip on me, down there, said it; she pulled me toward her, dragging me with her forceful hold.

My entire body lay on top of her. From the midpoint of our bodies where they were pressed against each other as closely as could be, when I came into her it was as if I woke her up. The skin around her eyes looked wet and her eyeballs rolled as she stared at me, moving her midsection up and down as if to insist on a rhythm I must follow too, as I moved up and down. That pair of spying eyes staring at us, from overhead this time, from some tiny hole in the ceiling that was the best vantage point, would be thinking that we must have reached the end, or that at least we were in the final stage of what we were doing. The woman under me trembled harder as she tried to hurry her climax. Here she was with her arms around my middle, pulling fiercely, pull- ing my whole body down.

XXI

IT AMOUNTED TO NOTHING MORE than a rushed attempt that went badly askew. I had to climb down and go back to exploring with my hand. She had stopped moving beneath me when she sensed me slowing down, lagging in the rhythm we had reached together. As I fell off her to lie next to her again, I realized she hadn't been at her climax after all, for she was able to come out of her frenzied state very quickly. She relaxed the hands that had been pressed tensely flat against my middle and slid them down to the mattress. Seeing me sit up, she began to look steadily at me, not bothered by the sight of my sex—damp, dangling loosely, once again limp. We had to go back to the beginning, understanding now that perhaps we had been too hasty that first time. Lying next to her, now I felt embarrassed by the pair of spying eyes. I no longer knew from what vantage point they were looking, where they were concealed. Because of those eyes I tugged the sheet up to cover the lower half of my body, but not the exposed body next to me, which was at once lifeless and expectant.

When I begin the next attempt—and I cannot wait long—it will be for the sake of the pair of spying eyes more than anything else. Perhaps, as we lie inert, those eyes are judging the time passing now as the final moment before we climb out of bed. But we must start all over again. We must begin at the very beginning and not from the point we reached. Not only that: it will have to seem as though we're seeing these two bodies for the first time, unclothed, exposed, naked. I reach my hand to her shoulder and touch her lightly, as if apologizing for something and also, with this one caress, firmly separating what we just did from what we will return to doing very soon.

But it turns out that returning to it—for a second round—is not slow and gradual. Between touching her shoulder and then slipping my hand lower on her body there were no fateful touches. This time it was like a test we would have to pass well and with no delays, as if it were a timed exam and speed was essential to our success. She was dry inside, as if her body had sucked in the moistness she'd had, or had sent it back, where it had been before, deeper inside. I knew, though, that my touch could make her go wet again in there. This time the woman had opened her eyes and she rested her head on her fist, in the pose of the thinker. Apparently my caresses, going deeper, were not coming close to that intimate pleasure of hers that closed her eyes and took her far away. She leaned her head on her fist as if she were thinking about something completely unrelated to what was going on down there at the very center of her body.

I knew I had to work quickly and return her to that state she'd been in, and so I figured I must redouble my speed because I was doing this alone. And then, her open eyes, dreamy and given over to whatever thoughts held them, pushed me to exert still more effort in an attempt to banish their obliviousness. I shoved my hand deeper inside, toward the wetness, which, just when it seemed I was almost there, eluded me, for she withdrew my hand and turned her body away. But I knew this was not the end. It was simply her complaint against our swift progress that was dragging her, against her will, out of her remoteness. I would be able to begin again after a pause, a space of detachment that she needed. I would begin by extending my hand, just like this, as if to placate her with a half-neutral, half-affectionate little touch.

The pair of spying eyes had widened, there somewhere overhead, in the ceiling. In her own way, the woman who had just bent her body away from me seemed to be in a state of preparation for this new round. She launched it hastily, as if the desire she was summoning back had returned suddenly, unexpectedly. Without any preliminary move she took my sex in both hands. She began pulling me toward her wetness, which seemed to have returned and must have welled up from its source somewhere deep inside. It was she who assumed control of this acceleration after that moment of rest she had wanted. As she began to quiver, one tremor following another rapidly, I knew I should abandon myself to her pace. My hands went to the dark aureoles on her chest, pressing hard on what lay below them, reckless enough to cause pain that would send the woman's voice all the way to the ears plastered to the other side of the door. No, I must not abandon myself completely to her tempo, just as I must be careful not to appear as if I am slowing down if she should go on ahead of me. I will remove myself just as I am reaching the pinnacle of my own onrush above her, just at that point, as if to deliberately delay our completion, after which we'll get up from the bed. I will make her follow my tempo as I move up and then down on her, and meanwhile I am recharging myself with the desire that keeps me pushing above her.

This time, too, the high wave that had borne me upward soon troughed. Immediately I lowered myself off the woman.

Trying to make me stay, pulling my body back toward her, she was apparently still a little way from reaching the pleasure she sought. When I lay back next to her she turned away from me to be alone as she went the small distance left on her own. But I restrained her, lifting her hand from where it lay and barricading that part of her body. I knew, though, that I must not leave her in this state for long. Without delay I must climb on top of her again to begin again where I had left off. If her wetness recedes or dries up this time it will no longer rise from those depths where it lies in wait.

But when we returned again to the point we had reached earlier, in our first try, we seemed unable to recapture the yearning that would press us together in a series of rapid shudders that pushed us on. Whatever it was that had urged us on then, now seemed to have fallen asleep in both of our bodies at once. Our movements seemed futile, and I began to imagine my body as if seeing it with the eyes that watched us furtively: how I would bend my body toward hers in order to lift myself and cover it, or how I would turn on my side to pull her to me. I envisioned my body, and imagined it, in its weak and passionless tossing. And beneath me or next to me, she would have her eyes open as if waiting for that wave of longing that had dwindled to come over her again, as suddenly this time as before. The spying eyes wherever they were in the ceiling were narrowed now as they accompanied us; perhaps now they were about to pull back from the peephole concealing them. No doubt they knew that the scene they had watched so furtively was at an end; and, as they withdrew before we did, that they were wiser than we were to the state we were in now. Or they knew now that being alone together in this room—me and the woman whose body I did not know, whose body I had memorized not at all—was not likely to bring us anywhere. It was a test, and the spying eyes knew, as they left the spot where they had secreted themselves, to descend rapidly to the rooms giving onto the room with the closed door, that they must show utter indifference as they focused on whatever ordinary object their gaze might encounter. The spying eyes would certainly reach the sitting room before we did, or the hallways, the spaces of departure and return. When she got up from the bed the woman's body sagged as if the only muscle keeping it together in a taut mass had gone limp, letting its parts dissipate. The woman returned to the body she inhabited when she was at home or on her outings with my mother, even if right now it lacked the clothes that normally covered it. Beginning to dress, she turned her face and body away from me, looking as though she intended to veil a nakedness whose exposure had been nothing but a mistake. So I knew, as I went over to my heap of clothes, that I must leave the room before she would. That way I could vacate the house quickly, emptying it wholly of me. We began putting on our clothes, backs to each other, and as I brought my belt up to my middle I thought how she would have to do her zipper up herself. I must leave the room first. Behind me she went over to the mirror on her table sitting next to the old bottles of perfume and began removing from her face, as far as I could tell, any trace that might still linger from our encounter. I must do that too; or, once outside, I must check on how I am looking and holding myself. I must not show anything that my mother—waiting in the sitting room or in a hallway leading to it—would notice. Or perhaps she would be waiting in our apartment, so that I'd be by myself when she saw me. Anyway, she could behave in exactly the same way even if she encountered me here—in the sitting room and not far from the door I would open, appearing as if I had done nothing and had not been where in fact I had been. She would turn toward me then, and as I walked over to where she stood she would straighten her back, and when I came up to her, she would give me her look, fierce and inquiring but nevertheless certain that when she turned I would follow her wordlessly to our home.

XXII

THAT INSINUATING LOOK, SIMULTANEOUSLY conspiratorial and slightly threatening: will it reappear, I wonder, on my mother's face? From my room, where I am either sitting at the table or lying on the bed beneath the little mirror, I can tell that she has left, closing the door hard behind her. I was not there waiting in her path in order to know whether she would give me her surreptitious signal. Since I had figured she would come by my room, when she didn't I felt myself sinking heavily into a morose anguish, even though I didn't know whether I wanted to go down there again if it were suggested to me.

I am in my room when she goes by on her way to the front door. If I were out there it would not be that arch, cajoling gaze that I would get, but rather a different look that lands on me as if to keep me frozen in place. A look I can see and judge: swift, sidelong, sweeping me from top to bottom; a gaze empty of questioning since there is nothing she needs to know. No, I will not be there in her path as she walks heavily toward the door. I remain in my room sitting at the table or lying on the bed. As for standing at the window, I hesitate, holding back as I wait for the heavy knot of disappointment and failure to dissolve and go away. And anyway, in here at this table of mine or on my bed, I am still exhausted from the weight of where I have been. I haven't rid myself yet of the body and skin that, naked, I was pressed against, lapping at its regions. It still feels attached to me in places; I cannot remove the edges that stick to me; I cannot release them. I will not be able to exchange this state of being for another by going over to watch whatever might happen below me, just beneath my window. Being alone with the woman in her room, I exhausted and emptied myself not only on her body but also on the body of her daughter, which, to give my body the energy it needed, I began to imagine in front of me or beneath me, glistening, slender and delicate and new, the foamy hair never shaved. I imagine it beneath me, a body inhabiting the woman's body or springing from it. What the two shared between them helped me along. The woman's hands were ripe with the body of her daughter from all the touching she did, all the massaging of those limbs. No doubt those hands would still pat that body into place, would wash it, stopping just where it curved, stopping at what it concealed. I was in need of this strong image, every bit of it, as I struggled to replace the body beneath me with a different body. Or to pull that body from hers, not only because she had touched and rubbed it, but also because her body had given birth to it, gave it up, emerging from that place clean of the traces of childbirth, as whole and raw and new as it was now.

I was still worn out by where my body had been. I must stay in my room, or in the house, but without my mother here. In the house, so that its hallways and tiles will cool me, or on the balcony where my father sits. As I approach, his head turns only the tiny distance he needs to focus his ear in the direction of the sound he senses coming toward him. He does not lift his head to be able to see me until I'm directly in front of him, and so it seems at that instant as if my appearance has taken him unawares, and it startles him. Even so, he gets up from his chair to greet me, leaning on his cane, which was another one of the items we had preserved among our old things. He asks if I want to sit down, because if so, he'll wait so we can sit down together, him on his chair and me on the chair facing it. I will do this for the sake of soothing myself. I need to spend my time in ways I'm used to in order to distance myself from where I have been. On the balcony as I sit down I feel more affection than usual for my father; I see him in tableaux from various moments in his past. Sit down . . . Sit down . . . he would say to me as we stood in his shop, so he could parcel out his attention between his work and me. Or I see him returning with the books whose titles I had written out for him on a slip of paper; as he proffers them, hoisting their weight, he has the look of finding it strange to carry anything except sacks holding goods from his store. Here! here are the books, he says to me and stands nearby while I look at them, one after another, asking me as I make my way through them whether he has gotten anything wrong.

I need to reestablish my sense of comfort and familiarity among the things I know, to fend off the state I was in and to drive it further away from me. Lying on my bed or pacing through the gloomy hallway where there is so little light, I decide that musing about the two women who sit below will tire me out and annoy me and weigh me down. Neither do I feel any desire to get up and go over to my pages to compare each line, after which I will turn them over, making new piles. I need to rest now, to remain flat on the bed or simply sitting at my table doing nothing. Or to return to my father out there on the balcony where he will get up slowly from his chair when my shape surprises him, to ask me whether I want to sit down; and I know that if I do sit down we will not talk about anything. He won't ask me any questions because he thinks I prefer that we remain silent and still. If he asks me where they have gotten to now, down there, I will appear grumpy, muttering in my irritation at being forced to return to speech that says nothing. They are working, I answer him in a way that lets him know he must not ask me what they're working at, just as he knows that if I answer a question about the work I do, I will not add anything to what he already knows. Nothing has changed, I will say to him, or I'll simply say that they have given me some new work to do. And so we remain silent when I sit down. Sitting on the balcony as he does has made him silent. That is what it has done, as if the words we used to exchange can be elicited only by coincidental, fleeting encounters in the hallway or kitchen, or at doors that stop us momentarily. It's his sitting on the balcony, his staying out there, that has silenced him. Do you want some water? he used to ask me whenever he saw me going into the kitchen. Do you want me to make you something? As if the words themselves arose from our chance meetings. Or as if he intended to pick up the water bottle to bring it for me, as I walked beside him, all the way to the door of my room where I would take it from him. He would be talking all the while, or he would seem, coming over to do these things for me, to be doing something hardly separate at all from his talking.

Sitting on the balcony has silenced him, as if by staying there through all the hours of his day he has separated himself. He has withdrawn from what goes on inside the house. He no longer even knows whether my mother is somewhere in the house or whether she has gone to visit her. From where he sits, there, his wrist draped on the balcony railing, he appears to have gotten as far away as he possibly can. He has gone to that final point after which lies nothing but the emptiness that separates us from the old city.

Still, he gets to his feet for me when he sees me directly in front of him, as if by standing up—and remaining standing—he is welcoming me there, to the place that has become his. He doesn't sit down again until I have decided to sit down, so that we sit down together. He has no words to say to me because he no longer moves around in the house doing anything that would generate the easy, passing conversation people have without meaning much of anything. Words like *It's hot* when he puts his hand on the pan and finds it hot. Or, noticing that someone else has gotten up and headed for the kitchen, *Sit down, sit down, I'll bring it, I will.* These are the sort of words he no longer says. And so we remain silent, sitting together on the facing chairs, and I resume thinking about whatever it was I was thinking of before I sat down. Or I go back to sweeping away whatever it is I want to erase from my head, giving myself over, as he does, to the breezes coming from below.

XXIII

THE LONG ROUTE I WALK lugging the pages I have tallied—a route I will retrace carrying another set of pages—is the only one I know in the confusion of streets that cut through the new city. Every time I take it I am affirming once again that it is my sole direction, and so I forget what I knew from my earlier wanderings. These are the only roads that exist, the only ones that are solid and real and that deposit me at that building where my feet know the way up. I have no reason to angle off onto any side streets, nor even to peer at what might be there in the blocks that lie beyond these little intersections. There is only the route between home and the building I know, the set of streets I regard as the straightest and fastest way to get me to where I must go. This is what my route becomes every time I walk it and affirm it as the only true route. But as I ponder my father's words, telling me I need to search for work in other offices, I realize how wrong I've been. My fixation on this route means that I have neglected all the other possibilities. If I am to act on his words, I will have to diversify. I will have to begin again, elbowing myself in among these jumbled streets, getting lost. But this is something I cannot do or don't want to do, since now, every time I leave our building, I already know how to proceed and what I will encounter with every step.

I will not change my route. I will not change my work, even though I know this means I'll go on with the very same tedium, replacing the pages I've checked with others I will check. But this resolution doesn't mean that I'm lulled by my father's assurance that tomorrow they will change my work. I'll go on doing the same thing, and I know that. In their tiny office I will get the same treatment every time, sitting patiently with my bundle of paper. The man inside will do the same thing every time: riffle through pages to see whether I deserve to be given more pages. I will not have any other work. The books I have read—those books for which I chose the smallest, most cramped space so I could isolate myself with them—will be of no help to me now. They did not teach me to do anything else. I read only old books. That's what the man sitting alone in the room where I had to wait for someone to leave before I could go in said to me. They were nothing but old books; one would lead me to yet another old book whose title I wrote down so that my father would bring it to me. Yes, they are old books, lined up in rows above where I sit. Gazing at them, my father seemed admiring and suspicious at the same time. He worried that something in the old pages or the dust seeping into them would surely sicken my body.

Old books, that's what they are, written by old people for people of old. I shouldn't have been satisfied only with them, said the man sitting at the large table that was too big for his narrow office. Then he handed me the packet of pages to match up, and I was aware again that this was the lowest level work among the various jobs they handed out here. My book reading was of no particular use to do this job, except that I had practiced reading and gotten used to spending time

sitting in front of pages and reading. That's the only help my
books gave me. When the man said that to me—about my old
books—I suddenly could see them in my mind's eye, a mass
of useless, cast-off, secondhand items. It took me no time to
believe him, because I had sensed the same thing myself. Not
only about the books I read but also about the clothes I ex-
tracted from the wardrobe to wear at home where no one saw
me except my mother and father. I felt old-fashioned, too,
when I thought about our old shop and how I would sit silent
and motionless among its goods. And also when it came to
my body: I am sure I look like people who used to exist but
who died before I could see or know them. I would not have
believed that man, who said these things to me, if I hadn't felt
this within me already. He did not tell me anything I didn't
already know, but he did make me aware of knowing it. You
haven't read anything but very old books, he said. He must
have seen that I was as close to ancient as the books I'd read.
He did not add anything to my knowledge of myself, but he
did get me right when he described my old books. I did not
simply take in this conviction; rather, I began to see his words
in everything I knew myself to be or to do. I am a person of
old when I sit on the balcony with my father—a scene that is
ancient, too. Every time I get up from the dining table, carrying my empty plate into the kitchen along with the pot that's
worn out from all the cooking it's seen, I am from another
time, a much older time. I am like that, too, when I go over
to lean on the windowsill, tipping my body over the edge of
it and hanging my head down. And I saw that in myself when
she looked up and saw me hunched over, waiting at the window above her. I looked as though I had always been there,
set down on a corner of the windowsill like a stuffed bird. It's
not that she happened to see me at the moment I appeared

there, but rather, that I had not moved. She would have had many chances to see me before this. That is everything my eyes said when hers happened to meet them. But she seemed to interrupt them by straightening up and turning away from their field of vision. No muscle in my face moved, and I showed no sign of having seen anything. I offered only that steady, unchanging gaze, even after she moved back from the window and walked slowly inside.

I was ancient, again, there at the window: she probably has no image of me except as a shadow that lurks at the angle of the window, hanging down and staring, whenever she has a passing thought about what is above her. The next evening I suddenly thought I should make sounds she could hear in her room. I should bang my window shut, and the sound would tell her that I was now behind the window and not tipping downward balancing on the windowsill. By closing the window—which means that later I will open it—I am creating a change of scene. I need to create sounds she will hear in her room. I need to close the window and then return to open it, to dispel what she saw when she craned her head to look above: a motionless shape, an image that doesn't change. And if I close or I open the window, that creates a sound that's close to her. It will reach her naturally, without any of those heavy echoes that sounds make when they come from rooms. It's like that when I make sounds she hears—I am erasing this look of the ancient that my silence and lack of movement have only enhanced. So now I'm making a commotion that seems to bring me forward, where sounds travel far, preceding me. Maybe I'll even give her a pleasant distraction, banishing the loneliness that permeates the outside world and from there invades her room, that space outside she's wary of and enters only rarely.

XXIV

DESPITE THE PASSAGE OF SO many years—thirteen now—they have done nothing in the old city since removing its residents. They have not put up one single building in any of those old quarters; they have not even built a road that would actually go anywhere. What I mean by *road* is one of those straight and wide boulevards where, it's said, they have finished the work underground—pipes and sewers and so forth—and have begun to work on the parts that will remain visible. I am talking about the sort of street that tells you from the way its route is cut what the city as a whole will look like. A thoroughfare that can be taken as a sign; seeing it, one would say: Here is the city center; there is the highway. But after all these years the only roads they have constructed are temporary ones, narrow and badly made, which will crack prematurely from rainwater and the weight of heavy trucks.

All my father needed to do to make himself comfortable, as he would say, was to hand over the little chest into my keeping. The money it held now was scant, and I saw as he held it out to me with both hands that perhaps he no longer liked to count it—were he even able to do so—since that would mean having to tell me something about what a bad state we were in. Or he would at least have to appear embarrassed as he gave

173

it over to me, there in his room with the door closed because he was so extremely cautious. But instead, he almost sprang up from the edge of the bed after depositing it in my hands. He began dusting off his hands and clapping them together to signal that a heavy burden that had exhausted him was now lifted. Or—and it was this that the days to come would confirm for me—he meant to say that now he had completed his last remaining duty by handing over the chest to me, and now he would be like a guest here among us for all the days that remained to him. My mother had already gotten there: in the rare moments she still spent in the house she did not go out onto the balcony to see him, even though she'd be close by as she passed the doors of the kitchen and dining room that looked directly out on him where he sat. During the day she now spent all her time down there, coming up only to pre-pare some item she needed—she and the woman—for what-ever it was they were doing. It got to the point where, coming in the front door that she left open, she wouldn't even glance over toward where my father sat, fully visible to her through the open doors to the balcony. As for him, most of the time he did not even know that she would have come in just now, or that she was in the apartment; when I sat with him he did not ask me whether she had come in or what she might be doing down there all day long, she and the woman. When she went out in the morning he never asked what she had cooked for us. He no longer took any interest in knowing what he was eating. At the table, as he sat staring at his empty plate, he did not know what dish would be set in front of him. In any case it wouldn't be anything much different from whatever we had eaten yesterday or on the days before that, for my mother had begun to cook every meal from the last one. She would add an eggplant to yesterday's leftovers or enhance them with a fried onion to alter the taste, along with the oil in which she had fried it. Once the food was on his plate my father hardly looked at it, only one brief inspection suggesting that he was more interested in testing the strength of his vision than in actually seeing the food. He wouldn't like it very much anyway, but he would not rise from it until he'd emptied his plate. It was a small portion my mother had cooked for us—for my father and me—adding something to what remained from yesterday's cooking. Despite that we would leave most of it in the pan, and we knew it would be part of tomorrow's meal. She cooks it for us, for my father and me, and shuts off the flame before hurrying downstairs, down there. My father does not ask me what she does all day long below, nor does he remark, in wonderment, that she is eating their food, which no doubt they cook together, she and the woman. He does not ask me anything about her or make any comment. When I begin to think he must be responding to her actions by feigning ignorance and staying silent, I watch him furtively to see whether he might be turning his head slightly toward where he thinks she is standing, or attempting a quick sly glance that might not tell him anything anyway. Or I keep a very close eye on him when I hear the sound of the door shutting behind her, to see whether her entrance jogs anything in him. When I see that the sound does not bring his head around, or that he gives no sign of the quick jerk of the head a person makes when they're surprised by something they were waiting for, I have the sense that he spends his time simply preparing himself to remain exactly as he is right now. I imagine that what gives him the ability to do that is his hatred of her, which no doubt consoles and entertains and stimulates him through all these daytime hours of sitting.

His hatred of her is what he needs most to give his body

the strength to sit unmoving all day long every day. It's what he needs to focus his attention, which otherwise might be smothered by the periods of oblivion brought on by the breezes coming from below. It is what he needs to strengthen his eyes under the dense film that covers them. With the loathing that braces and protects his body, his eyes put up a resistance to the thick pale film, and their blackness shines from beneath it like the face of a drowned person that floats just beneath the water's surface. I almost want to say to him: It's her over there. Hate her. She is there at the door; she has put out her hand to open it. She is there even though she won't give you even a single glance, as if you are not even here. . . .

I am almost ready to tell him to hate her in order to rid him of his fatigue and the restless irritation of afternoon. Then, sitting across from him, I see that his eyes have already grown weaker and I know when he raises them toward me that he sees me as if through a layer of muddy water. It must tire him, I think. It would be better for him to close his eyes and summon the clean and sharply outlined images that no doubt his memory has preserved. It would be better for me, too, since I would no longer be suffocating under the weight of imagining things the way his eyes convey them to him. In that state of fatigue, in the weariness of afternoon, his eyes look as though they've brought him nearer to his end. His eyes are how I have measured the strength remaining in him. His eyes have become the distinguishing mark of his body, its barometer, now that he no longer walks or even moves. In the afternoon hours their blackness—which gave him whatever vision he had—has paled to a wan gray: the blackness and not the film over it. At those times I see him as very close to his end. Perhaps he knows that, I will think, and no longer cares whether I'm sitting across from him. He gives me no sign, no indication of interest, when I look as if I'm about to get up. He knows it, he sees it in himself, in these stretches of restlessness and fatigue when he asks me the question that I know he's pulling up from somewhere other than the place where his cache of everyday phrases resides. Where have they gotten to now, down there? he asks and cranes his head forward. When I respond by saying that they are still working to level the ground where I can see nothing rising, he inclines his head to me as if to say something that he realizes instantly there's no point in saying.

But I know what he is keeping himself from asking: Can I see anything clearly at that distance, where they are? When I add that they have collected their bulldozers and trucks in one central spot, I'm answering the question he didn't ask, while at the same time I'm leading him to hope that they are actually getting ready to erect something. But this doesn't excite his curiosity, nor does it bring him up out of the weariness to which he has reverted. That's because their lackadaisical pace in razing the old city will keep the bulldozers and trucks there where they are, waiting to begin, and nothing will begin. If it does, it will be for someone else and not for him; the film over his eyes will not slow down to give him time to see any of what they will have built in the end.

The film over his eyes will not allow him the time to see for himself what they will build: not only his shop, which he stopped mentioning some time ago, but not even any of the roads or buildings he knows there. Here is our shop, look, it's right over there, he would say in the days soon after our move, believing he would return to it after a bit more time had passed, and he would find that nothing had changed except that it looked newer now, after the work they had promised to do. In the years gone by since our move he has gone on believing that they would simply give new life to the city by razing it and rebuilding it as it was before; once again, he would be going from home to his shop, passing through streets and by shops he knew from before, except that they would all be newly rebuilt.

The bulldozers and dump trucks clustered there in a near-central spot will be waiting a long time before they are put in motion. He will not be able to see anything rising above the places and things that he would recognize if only he could see them. Their long delays, this protracted period that seems so deliberate, will not give him enough time, just as the film over his eyes will not wait for him. Now I know, in this time we spend together, that the film over his eyes will not let him see any building high enough that to see all of it one must get a certain distance away.

XXV

I HAD ALWAYS SUPPORTED MYSELF by pressing my body against the wall just at the side of the window frame in order to best conceal myslf, but now I was able to stand leaning against the center of the window itself, gazing however I liked toward the window below me. I could even make a noise deliberately by flinging open the window panels so that they would knock against the wall before swinging out slightly again. That lets her know that I am here, so she'll come nearer, but also so she will feel at home with the stretch of lonely sand beneath her rather than being frightened by it. Sometimes when she knows I am directly overhead she stands for a long time just below and raises her head once or twice to see if I am still there. Or she twists and arches her body to look up as she's getting ready to head inside, away from her window. I am there when she looks; she sees me at the instant she twists, as if I have responded to her motions by stretching my head further toward her, looking at her as she does at me. But it's only a fleeting instant, a brief glance ended by her equally swift withdrawal as she heads inside. An instant; it is not enough for my face to change expression, to move from that first gaze that had not even yet formed. But I

179

know she did curve toward me, or at least toward my window, and not only to see that I was there but also so that I would see her—I, who stand there just as she does.

In that fleeting glance all she sees of me is my face, which I imagine she already knows. She must know my body as well, which is hidden below the window now, because she must have seen me walking along the sand track with the canvas bag hanging from my shoulder. Or she might be present when they—the woman and my mother—talk about me. She knows about me, she must, but even so, she comes back to the window another time, knowing I am still there. And when she comes back she stands there for me, for my sake, as if she's giving me extra time to look at her or lengthening the opportunity for which I have waited. She stops there; she stands for me, pressed against the windowsill so I can see her grave expression as she looks out on the sand that I know doesn't fully occupy her attention. She is showing herself to me; and so the way she stands is the way she wants to be seen, her arm flung across the windowsill or her head lowered to tell me she is looking down.

Or she does that for her own sake, and so as she exposes herself to me she's responding to what it is that makes her stand naked before the wardrobe mirror or walk, naked as well, through the house whose rooms and passages have emptied out for her. She is bringing that to completion by standing here for me, by looking at me with that quick, passing glance she throws my way—this look that is to remain swift and glancing, this look that is all she needs to know that I am there waiting above her.

This look of hers won't change, and will only let her see that I am still there. Still, she must finish what she has begun. She will reveal something of her body, and then she will expand on that to reveal more. For her to begin and then to quicken her pace, I must get her out to the balcony once, and again and again, opening the shutters to their widest so that they bang against the wall to make the sound she hears, and toward which she will turn.

I lie in wait above for the time to come in which she begins to reveal to me what she already reveals to herself. She will not stay here standing like this, her arm along the windowsill as if giving observers plenty of time to satisfy their desire to look. Here in front of the window, she will certainly do some of what she does in front of the mirror. She won't be taking a chance that someone would see her from the other edge of the sand because the mounds of it do not end in anything. There at her open window she will be as hidden as if she's in her room behind her wardrobe doors. No one but me will see her, and I will be like one of her mirrors, among which she moves whenever the house has emptied itself for her. A mirror I will be, one of her mirrors, and she will not be afraid, appearing to me, because she thinks that anyone like me is bound to remain silent and still in front of what he sees. I will make no sound; I will not move. Nothing more than standing there at the window, returning once again to the side of it, to watch secretly, to steal this which is offered to me, as if to be sure that no one knows of me.

XXVI

WHEN THE WINDOW PANELS OPENED at that late hour of the night, causing a screech that didn't come to an end even when the window was entirely open, I did not know if by doing this she was summoning me to come near or to arise from my sleep if I happened to be in bed. She was standing there in the light that poured from her room as if the late hour made it brighter and stronger. Her sleeplessness had gotten her out of bed and here she was below me, the signs of her struggle with it intact. Her nightgown was crumpled and damp with her sweat, slipping slightly off her shoulder, which I could see as far as her upper arm. Her hair, which she had kept tied back, made an unusually wide puffy halo around her face, which was usually covered by it and which I had not yet seen plainly, always having to look from above. She had not been summoning me by opening the window and letting the screech of it reverberate, I thought. I even thought for a moment that in opening the window as she had, she showed that she was still immersed in her fury and oblivious of anything else. As if this—her ire—is the moment when she is serious, is the truth of her. As if standing there for me, earlier, had been just a game or a pastime, and this moment, now, was not the time for any of that.

But I do not have to withdraw, retreating into my room. This time of night is one she does not know; she doesn't know how to be at this late hour. Indeed, it won't be long before she realizes she's afraid of it. And then she'll look to where I stand overhead. I need not retreat inside and distance myself from this moment of her anger. I ought to stay standing here. For this is my hour, this hour in which she awoke, and so I must remain here where I stand, for at this hour I can do what I cannot do at other times. The emptiness and the silence that extend across the sand are at their strongest—now, in this hour of her sleeplessness. There is nothing but me here, close by, as close as any two people with a wall between them can be; and there is no one here but me.

This is my time, in which I know how to be. I will not withdraw, retreating inside, and I won't bring my head back or move to the side of the window. I will stay as I am, waiting for her to raise her head toward me, which will happen once her thoughts set her down where she is used to me standing, here above. I will remain where I am and as I am, looking at her howsoever I like, to let her know, when she turns to me, that I have been here looking at her like this the whole time. I won't flinch when it looks as though I'm stealing a furtive look at her bare shoulder where, even at this distance that lies between us, I can see the gossamer blonde hairs, as if the falling beams of light have magnified them. It won't be long before she raises her head toward me. There are not many things in front of or around her that would excite her gaze. I know that very very soon indeed this is what she will do and that she will not return to her room before she does it. This hour in which she has awoken is mine. That is, I know what will happen in it. This hour is my time. And as I wait for her to turn toward me I will be calm, fully and happily engrossed in staring at her bare shoulder and her feet, shoeless on the tile floor and bare, her big toes visible, held slightly apart from her other toes and from the two red patches that her slippers conceal but also create, where they press in on her feet.

She was leaning her elbows on the windowsill when she lifted her head to see if I was there. She did it with a sudden movement, just like that, as if in response to a sound escaping that would alert her to me. She saw me there, framed by the strong beam of light coming from her room, my head and body straining forward. I expect she even saw my eyes gleaming in the light as I looked at her or toward where her eyes moved once they had shifted from me. I was very quiet and calm, in possession of myself, of my standing here and looking, leaving to her to decide what to do in the circumstances. Perhaps she understood that this time she must do something different, and so she did not look away immediately. As she gazed at me she was thinking about what she'd do next. But that didn't last long: only moments, and then she stepped inside. But she withdrew slowly, deliberately, as if demanding time before responding to an urgent call coming from the other end of the room.

As she stepped back she went on looking at me, as if to tell me to wait here for her return. She did not do anything once she had gone in; she didn't go any farther than the door of her room. All she did by going inside was interrupt the moment we were in, ending it so we could begin a new moment. She did not even comb or pat her hair that fluffed around her face like a big circle. She didn't put on her slippers to cover her bare feet. And as soon as she came back to the window she had her head raised toward me to see me there, where I had brought my head and body even further forward outside the window, but without looking uncomfortable or distressed by this seemingly awkward position. This time she hadn't come to the window to look outside at the night sky and the sand, but rather to stare at some point in the window frame in front of her. Standing at an angle not facing directly outside, resting her arm along the length of the windowsill, she looked as though she was preparing for a long stay and positioning herself so she could look at me without having to twist around or to the side. This way I could see the front of her—chest and belly and all the way down to her feet. Likewise she could look at me merely by raising her eyes, but I was sure she wouldn't do more than that until I took the next step. And I must do it quickly, while she is standing there like that, preparing for me. She won't go any further or add anything new until I begin; it's as if she changed position in order to see what I would do in response. Now, while she's looking out at the vistas framed by the open window, tipping her head slightly upward so I can see it haloed by the circle of her hair, I must say something. I must say something she will hear. For the next step—the one I must take—cannot be anything else. I must say something she will hear. When I say it I will be performing the first obvious, unmistakable act, the kind it is difficult to extract oneself from—unlike a simple, brief glance—because its nature is deliberate. The words I must say as the first and undeniable step which— after I have said them—might reveal another truth about all of these glances and the repeated moments spent standing behind the window. The words, when I say them, will not allow subterfuges or evasion because the moment they are uttered they'll produce an immediate and unalterable effect. And afterwards, after I say them, she cannot go on standing there exactly as she does now. The voice she hears addressing her might surprise her into anger, and she might slam the windows shut with quick and furious hands. There is nothing certain about her glances, whether the quick looks or the slower gazes. Nothing sure in the way she stands and leans like that out of the window, which brings her body closer to me. If this happens it will be like a series of images in quick succession that one's fancies and suspicions string together, only to chase them away or to erase them altogether. That is something else I must put an end to, by speaking. By saying the words I have readied myself to say, not only waiting to say them but also to hear them myself, coming out hoarse, constricted, sounding peculiar as if they have emerged from a throat that belongs to someone other than me. But I must say them and I must do so quickly, for by now she may have reached the very end of this interlude when she stands here below me. I must say them, now, before some movement of hers indicates she is about to go. Now, before I let that moment go, before the moment comes when her patience is exhausted, now . . . I must . . . now. . . .

I've been waiting for you. I knew you would get up out of bed.

She did not lift her eyes to me until after the sounds—all of them—had floated down to settle around her below, hoarse and shaky, as if before arriving they had crossed a long patch of rough ground. My hesitation and clumsy bashfulness must have slowed their descent, for even I heard my voice only as it arrived, or as she heard it—I seemed to hear it long after I actually said it. But those words of mine did arrive, all of them, to settle over her like something heavy that kept her eyes—now turned this way—fixed on me, seeking an explanation and asking a more open question at the same time. When she jerked her head to signal that she did not understand, I knew she was doing it to keep the awkwardness of the situation on my shoulders alone. She would require another onslaught to move her another step forward. This, also, I must do.

I knew you would get out of bed, would leave your tossing and turning. I waited for you so you wouldn't be alone.

XXVII

DESPITE THE MANY YEARS THAT have passed, they still haven't erected anything I can actually see from our house, such that I could say to my father: Now they have begun. But they are building something there. In the mornings, before fatigue caught up with him and made him drowsy, he would say to me in a tone that conveyed both a question and an answer, not to mention a complaint: They are still at the same point there . . . everything is still where it was? He had stopped telling me I must go there to see what they were doing. Now, and over the past stretch of time, he has altered how he says this, so as not to appear quite so insistent, since that annoyed me. Instead, he would say to me, If one were to go there he would see it with his own eyes. Or he might remark that it was likely, now, that they were putting down the foundations of buildings, all of them at one go, but he figured you could only really see this at close range. But now he had stopped saying these things to me using any of his circuitous routes. He also simply stopped the wave of questions that, like his earlier ones, could have been voiced had his boredom and weariness not silenced him. Only two or three times did he say to me, revealing the wrath that accompanied him constantly in his silence: But they must leave marks on the ground! That way they would know how the streets were placed, so they would know how to cut them again. This he stopped repeating before he reached the point where he no longer cared; for to say it again, he would have to also tell me to go there to see whether they had done any of this at all.

He stopped telling me to go there. He knew that time would not last long enough to allow him to see anything finished, even if they were to announce today that they had begun pouring the foundations. He could no longer bear the waiting, either. For years he had waited, and he felt he had been abandoned again and again, his hopes forsaken over and over. Instead of demanding that I go down there he had begun to say to me—in the period before this final silence of his—that I should go over *here*. He meant the new city and he indicated it by retracting his hand slightly and redirecting it toward where the new city would lie, behind him. He wanted me to go there so that I would get to know the people whom—he would always add—I could not afford not to meet. I would understand that he had in mind those who worked arranging matters that people could not arrange for themselves.

In the first months following our move, when he would go around in the new city getting acquainted with what was there, none of the men he knew had died yet, obliging family and friends to organize a funeral. Making his circuits, he never saw even a patch of ground which—he could be re-assured—would be left empty for those who would die here before they could return to the old city. He wanted me to go and meet these people, to find out where they were and to see the cemetery, so I would know where it was. You must go! he would say to me, showing his irritated impatience that most of the time lay just below the surface, irritation at how I satisfied myself with that single route I took carrying the pages I had finished matching up. In his anger he seemed to be hastening my going there, for perhaps what he was anticipating would take us by surprise. Perhaps, especially if he remained this upset, it would come quicker, shortening the life allotted to him by fate.

I knew it was my duty to handle many tasks as we waited for it to happen, things beyond simply going there to make their acquaintance. The money in the little chest had dwindled so far—very few paper bills remained inside—that it was no longer worth hiding the box or keeping a watchful eye on it. The meager sums I gleaned from collating the piles of paper wouldn't cover the cost of a shroud, let alone a grave. Even before I got that far, I was worried that merely going to those people and getting to know them would cost me something, perhaps more than the chest held now. Even just going to them—since I would have to try out new routes and spend more time out of the house—might require money. You must go to see them, he began repeating, but his intonation suggested that he was asking me whether I had gone already, or even that he rejected the very thought that I might not have gone yet. The filmy layer that had transformed his eyesight had thickened even more; only two tiny pinpoints remained uncovered, like slits that each faced in different directions, fleeing from each other. Looking at me he would tilt his head to try to align the images he saw in one eye with those in the other. Not only (I thought) did he see me as if I were covered by a filmy substance or enveloped in a fog but also, he saw only a tiny patch of me through these pinholes.

It was not the waning of his eyesight I was seeing: it was his death. That is what I saw in his eyes, and it crept forward noticeably day by day. Since I knew he was watching it as closely as I was, and that he knew what it meant as well as I did, I could see that he was putting me in a position to say to him, Tomorrow I will go. I said it just like that, without any further explanation, as if we had already agreed on what it meant and what we would do. Tomorrow I will go, I said to him, as if to reassure him that we would get through this task without any anxiety. After I said it, he turned his face away toward the breeze coming from below. He seemed to need a moment by himself to swallow this unnamed thing we had now agreed to take care of. In streets I do not know, I will have to search for places I don't even know how to recognize. These were not simply the shops and offices of people who arrange the personal affairs of other people; they were other places still, different ones, places he might be able to name for me, those which I imagined sold or rented what was need-ed to prepare the dead. But the little chest did not contain money enough to allow me to prepare for this, to make ready what we would need.

Over there, I would also have to search for shops where they bought old items. From the collections in the shops I might be able to tell what I could sell from among our be-longings and furnishings. Rather, I could see what things I should sell first, since in times to come I would be selling other things. I knew now that the first to go would be my fa-ther's bed, his wardrobe, and whatever was left of his personal effects. But for the moment I would go to see what they were buying, there in the shops that I did not know how to find or to recognize when I found them. When I returned from this errand, I would have to handle things on my own because my father would not even pay attention to where the com-motion was coming from, made by the men who would shift around the big pieces of furniture and take some of them away. My mother would not be here, and when she did come back she might do no more than look hard at the spaces now emptied of her things, shaking her head sarcastically as she went into the kitchen or to her room to get whatever she had come for. She no longer had any interest in what happened here. She might even enjoy seeing belongings removed from where they had always been. It might relieve her to see that we were taking measures in the house without her, and she might relish seeing the appearance of the house change with the removal of his things. She would probably think it was the perfect opportunity for a certain resident to relinquish her accustomed role. As it was now, she no longer did anything for us before going out, except her scant cooking, and all that meant was adding another ingredient to the pan. Leaving the kitchen, she left the double doors open wide as if to say that this completed her work. As if to remind us that she was do- ing this work for us, for me and my father. She would no longer eat what she cooked here. The two of them, she and the woman, ate something else. Cooking it, they were enter- taining themselves as if preparing food for their outing. From the window of the empty bedroom I watch the two of them walking down the sand track, for now their excursions involve going to the new city. I see them from the back as they walk. They do not talk and they look to me as though they are head- ed to some place where they're expected. From that distance I can see the woman's legs, skin containing their flesh and flattening it out delicately. I begin following the white skin of her legs to the places in her body that her clothing hides. Or her body is revealed to me in the movement of her buttocks as each one lifts in turn. Every time I see her walking I begin to imagine or remember her body, which I know, still naked, for her clothing does not succeed in covering it: naked and white, smooth but erupting and billowing in places, since her plumpness is not distributed evenly.

Her clothes don't cover her when I watch her, just as her gait along the sand track does not erase her image, silent on the bed, mute as if from embarrassment and pain together. I see them leaving, she and my mother, and I cannot believe that over there in the new city they'll be content to sit silently, doing nothing. Since they're not talking to each other they look as if they're intent on hurrying to something that awaits them. I think it's likely that my mother, whose wide shoulders remain steady and her head high as she walks, succeeded in finding someone for the woman with whom—on his bed there in the new city—she duplicates the painful embarrassed silence that I know. And no doubt my mother will be hovering there, as she did here, her heavy body pacing outside the room with the closed door as if she has something to occupy her other than simply waiting.

From the window of the empty bedroom I see them coming back. They spent exactly the same amount of time there as they do every time. They did not lose their way or follow a different route that would take them somewhere new. They go to one and the same place, every time they go out. They do not change their route, because if they did, they would have to label what they do as a bit of play, just something to pass the time.

XXVIII

THE SMALL TRUCK ADVANCING SLOWLY and precariously up the sand track might have been a fugitive that happened to swerve off course and come here. No truck or car had traversed the sand track since the two old people on the ground floor left with all of their belongings. The feet tamping down the track in their rare journeys back and forth didn't harden it or even make it level. The truck swayed constantly as it approached, and then swung around with a screech. When it stopped and backed up to align its rear end with the wide main entryway, the sound it made seemed excessive for this little maneuver. From the window where I stood I saw the top of the cab and the empty truck bed behind it. There was no one in the building except me, no one to look out his window in annoyance, no one who might need to pass through the entryway that the truck had blocked. The two women had gone out to the new city as usual and would not return before their usual time, which I knew was just before the return from school of the one they would be waiting for after their own return. As for my father, he would remain sitting where he always sat, keeping his back to the sand track despite the loud screech that he must have heard. Nor, a few moments later, would he turn his face in the direction of the front door where the two men appear, turning without delay into my room. I lead the way, and then I stand nearby while they take the books down from their shelves.

They take these old books that I have neglected, leaving the dust to cover the edges of the pages and other exposed surfaces. The dust mixes with grains of sand that whip in when the breeze comes up, and which I used to remove whenever it occurred to me to take down some books from where they sat. I did that just for the sake of running my eyes over them, one book and then another, that's all, just like my father did with his money, counting and rearranging it. Lately I had neglected them as they sat there on the shelves. Even the two men, who were surely not so concerned about dust, stepped closer to the open window so that when they blew off a layer of dust it would fly outside. Or they slapped the heavy old book covers and flaps to remove the sticky specks that they couldn't blow away. Only then, once they thought the book wouldn't soil the hands of whoever would be picking it up next, they added it to those they had already piled on the table. Standing near them, or between them, I saw myself taking down books just as they did, an armful at a time, beginning at one end of a shelf and looking only at how dusty or how thick a book was. I was just like them now, or almost. Whenever I happened to see the title of one of these books, perhaps one lying atop the pile, which they had not stopped adding to even though it had begun to sway, I paused only momentarily, remembering my father as he presented it to me, his face still sweaty from walking quickly, as he always did. It was nothing more than an ephemeral image in my head, in which I saw myself sitting on that chair, there in my father's shop, turning the book over in my hands and sniffing the fragrance of ink and paper. Or I remembered picking it up where it lay open, face down on the low table in the hall-way between the doors in our old home. But such memories didn't hold me for long. These were nothing but insubstantial wafts of memory that passed rapidly as one of the two men covered the book with another book placed on top of it, or when one of them reached to remove a clutch of books from the very highest shelf that they had not yet finished emptying.

As the pile of books grew higher, it seemed to me that I was tucking these flashes of memory in among them, sending them along—with the books—to the truck. Ever since I had begun working on the identical sets of pages, I had gotten into the habit of sitting at the table so that all the books were at my back—these old books that as I read them did not equip me with anything but their decrepitude. The books, all of them! I said to the two men as they paused under the shelves asking where they were to start. All of the books, I said: all of those old books, which (now I can see, as I see myself reading them in the narrow hallway between the doors) made me into the image of a boy who had already grown old and decrepit. The surface of the table was completely covered now with books they had removed from the two highest shelves where, now that they were emptied, I could see the wall, darkened and dingy from its long concealment. My mother used to say that staying among books would make me ill because she imagined my body would be desiccated by their constant company. The books, all of them . . . which now, after dust-ing them off, the men had begun to pile on the bed. Those books that they won't carry downstairs until all of them are off their shelves and piled in batches on the table, floor and bed.

I leave the room as they're taking down the last books. I leave so they can move among the piles they've made. Wait-ing behind the door, I keep my head filled with the image of the wall, but without the dark color framed by the shelves that make it even darker. I think about how it might be possible to rid the wall of that stain of darker color if a broom or a big towel were taken to it. The shelves as well, I said to the men as they clapped their hands together to rid them of the last particles of dust sticking there. The shelves, and the desk, I said. They could take the shelves down as easily as they had removed the books from them.

XXIX

NOW THE ROOM HAS GROWN large and weightless, released from the possessions that had burdened it. The men moved the table I kept for working on the pages to the corner behind the door. My bed remained as it had been, at the center of the room, but it was no longer hemmed in. The room had become light. Emptied of books and shelves, the wall had gone back to its original pale color, which had required only a bit of sweeping. The two men had done that as well before they went away.

The room has become weightless, and in it, I am airy and clean and new as well, like a light reflected by a gleaming metallic surface. Like the light flowing from the lamp hanging from the high ceiling to brighten the room cleanly and evenly, for there are no books to darken or obstruct it. There is no longer anything in the room to weigh me down, tugging one side of me toward it when I am standing still or moving around, pulling part of me away from the rest. Now I can leave or enter the room without feeling the slow heaviness of what I had always thought of as a vast and decisive threshold separating going out from coming in. As I stand behind the window looking toward the one I see below me or waiting for her to come, I sense the open space at my back stretching out

199

far behind me. Not just the room; it's the entire house, and now I leave my door open. I feel it all behind me, open to me, now that it has been emptied by my mother's departure, and my father is always seated in the same place out there on the balcony, huddled against the railing.

Now I can do as she does when she stands for a time at the window and then goes away for a spell to the roomy interior where she moves around. I am no longer simply waiting there in the one spot where I stand, but rather it's as if—walking as she does through the rooms—I'm following her, tracing her footsteps exactly along the squares of tile just above her head. When the two women have gone out, or on the occasions when they are late to return, I think about how we—the two of us, she and I—are free together in these two wide-open spaces, one directly above the other. Stepping exactly as I think she has just stepped, I feel I have come very near to her, my body has grown so close to hers that both take the same step on the same square of tile at the same time.

It is her bare feet that take these steps—feet sticky with sweat from her shoes so that every time she tries to lift them from the shiny, polished tile it's more like she's sliding than stepping. So it's the sound of the tacky soles of her feet parting slowly from the tile that rises to me, though I can barely hear it. As I follow that whispery sound I know it will take me, after making its wandering circuit, to the window, where she'll be peering out with her body leaning forward so that her face is lifted toward mine. I will have arrived just as she does, and I will have turned my face downward. We are alone, like this, in the two homes that sit one atop the other. We move exactly as we please in each and then we turn to the pair of open windows. I see her when I get there, turning her face toward me, just as I can see—if I lean my body some distance outside the window—her bare feet and legs emerging thinly from the anklebones and rising to where they will finally become rounded. They have changed, or at least they have made strides toward this change whose completion I think they have not yet reached. I see her face near to me and I imagine that it, too, will likely undergo that change which, as fast-paced as it is—altering now one part of her and now another—seems to veer unpredictably in a new direction from one day to the next. Or the process of change is particularly strong one day and something in her changes visibly, but it slows the next day and she looks more the way she did before. Sometimes I see it happening in her eyes: looking at me, they appear to have hardened, become more merciless; or they seem to be scrutinizing what they stare at more closely.

And I know that this look will not remain there, for these constant alterations will return her gaze—after the wave settles into calm—to the hesitant, waiting look that her eyes held before. Or when, like her, I retreat from the window and begin, like her, to wander through the rooms, I return her to her earlier self in which the raw wind of change has brought no more than tiny ripples of newness as yet. I imagine her feet falling small and fresh onto the tiles, still showing the delicate swelling that covers the ligaments. But I know, as I imagine her this way, that she has already changed, not only from what my eyes can take in but also from what is being brought forth inside of her, where I cannot see. But in fact I see both at once, for her eyes would not have hardened like this or grown more penetrating, holding fast onto the object at which they stare, if it were not for the whirling buffets of wind whose hot gusts rise from beneath those eyes, disturbing and ruffling them. When the hot wind calms, settling into stillness, it leaves traces that will not go away. The fuzz above her upper lip will not disappear now that it has formed into a downy moustache. Her face, molded and fired by the blasts of wind, will retain something of their heat after the calm descends. I must hurry. It's not enough that I stand at the window leaning toward her while she looks up at me, or that I circle with her among the rooms, listening intently for her movements through them. I must hurry, for in just a little while the change will take her away from what she is now and steer her toward how she must behave with the new appetite she has developed. It will teach her how to hide these yearnings away so that she can reveal them when she feels the time has come. I must hurry. I must take that great step, there in her home when it's empty, or here in our home that my father and mother have emptied, each in their own way. Or even on the stairs, in the space that keeps us apart. In the darkened space whose only light is that which filters in from outside. It will be empty as well; we won't need to watch out for anyone coming, except from one direction: when the two women return, ascending from their walk and making noise that we'll hear for some moments before they draw near.

I must hurry to get there ahead of a new way of being that waits for her, and that I know she'll inevitably reach. When she gets there, she will not be satisfied with hiding her desire in order to act on it when she wishes. No: when she gets there, and when I see her going out onto the sand track, it will be as if she's hiding something in her gait, something that takes her to a place that offers her no rest, there in the new city.

XXX

THE BODY I SAW AND knew naked: these clothes have not succeeded in covering it up, nor has the passage of time been able to erase it since it appeared to me naked, that one time. Each time I see the woman going out, she and my mother, walking along the sand track, her bare skin is revealed to me beneath her clothes. And as she moves I can see how her buttocks rise, one and then the other, naked, and I assume that with every motion the whole side of her body lifts too. Whenever I imagine that, I feel in complete sympathy with the woman who seemed as if she couldn't manage her body very well on her own. Next to her on the track was always my mother, shoulders broad, walking with nothing in her body moving but her legs. They didn't talk, she and the woman, as they went, nor did one of them ever turn to the other, as if they were going not for the sake of amusing themselves but to accomplish something they knew, in a place they knew. Reaching the end of the sand track, they never turned around to glance at what they were leaving behind. The woman walking next to my mother, silent and obedient, has no fear of being out late, leaving her daughter alone in the house. They believe, she and my mother, that the building is protected by its isolation and the open stretch of sand surrounding it.

Inside, there is no one but me and my father, and neither of us, as the woman and my mother both see it, can do any harm or cause any fright.

Or, watching the two of them walking, I would wonder whether they might have something in common to do there in the place they've made their destination, but I don't know what share in it each one has. The time the woman spends in bed in the room behind the closed door will see my mother simply waiting behind that door, just as it was that time when I was in there with the woman, behind the closed door to her room. I do not know what my mother's aim is in going with her, in going together to wherever it is they go. As for the woman, I don't suppose that she is doing what she does because she desires or has chosen it. They have this something to do in common, but I don't know what share each one has in it. When I see them returning late it occurs to me that one of them is giving pleasure to the other when both bow to a single longing, normally felt by one woman. It occurs to me also that they do the same thing when they sit for hours silently in their outings to the edge of the sand.

They go out every day, leaving the two homes behind them. Since these days they're usually late in returning, they must be spending considerable time getting to know places they'll turn to if they tire of the place they go to now. When my mother leaves, as when she returns, I have begun to imagine that my father, despite the state of oblivion that possesses him most of the day, has retained a blazing hot crater in his head, no bigger than a fingertip but glowing red hot, still aflame amidst the ashes accumulating around it. He has done this as if he knows that her leaving us—which began when he was still capable of hearing and seeing—has gone to extremes now. He has surely kept that reddened pit glowing like a tip of hot iron, and whenever I see him sitting out there, head dropped to his chest as he naps, I think that what I've imagined inside his head, flaming and alive, does not help him, but rather intensifies his fatigue. This is because he cannot put it out at will. When I awaken him to eat, carrying his plate out to where he's sitting, I sense that something inside him has not allowed him to take a truly restful doze. Despite that, I feel I should go on waking him, even just to see him raise his head slowly and move his tongue around to moisten the dryness in his throat. Here's the food, I come out to tell him, once and then again. Here is the food, I say to him, to let him know where to look for the plate. Here—this is the spoon, I say, so that he will put his hand out in my direction to take it. I start talking to him, trying to get him to wake up enough to eat. I try for a state of alertness that will not suddenly reverse and return him to his napping. Eat, Papa, I say to him. He lowers the spoon to the plate of food that I have to steady, lest it slip from the tray and fall to the floor.

He won't eat much anyway. Three or four attempts, tiny bites, and then he stops, leaving the spoon on the plate where he has set it down. Before I lift the tray from him I say, just as I do every time: You haven't eaten anything today, you must eat. But I know that he doesn't need any more than the portion he took. His body does not need more than that, since he does nothing and no part of his body moves. I can see that even his breathing is minimal, as slight as the food he swallows; as soon as he's done eating he returns to his napping, and to that blazing crater that makes him ache even when he is asleep.

For we have left him here all alone where he sits, at the balcony railing near the air that descends to the old city, bringing him with it. We left him there alone, my mother by distancing herself more every day until now she is almost never here, and I by standing at the window or pacing through our rooms readying myself to go back to the window. In the hours when I work on the pages I find myself more aware of his presence, and I am more attentive; I get up whenever I've finished three pages, or maybe four, to look in on him and then to ask him, Do you want anything, Papa? Can I do anything for you? On days when I go out to submit the piles of paper I have finished matching up, I put the water bottle on the balcony wall and I move his cup closer to him after filling it with water so that at least it will be easy for him to take his first sips. He may not need any more, since his constant dozing leaves him unaware of how dry his throat is. Do you want anything before I go? I ask him, so that he can tell me if he wants me to help him with his bodily needs, or if he wants to do it himself but while I am still here and can wait for him. I figure that before I leave I must prepare him for a half day on his own, during which I'll be imagining him—over that stretch of time—as he slides farther and farther down in his chair until he is all but falling on the floor as he naps. I begin to walk faster along this route I know so well. To banish from my mind the way I must look—my fast walk which is more like hopping, and I know I look to others as if I'm about to stumble and fall—I think about finding him fallen, having toppled onto his face, but then I think that thanks to my hurrying, I will surely catch him in time.

After I arrive I don't stand there long with him, only long enough to ask my questions, which I am always careful to pose even though I know they're not likely to permeate his dozing or awaken him. When I go back to my room to take off my outdoor clothes, for a moment I think that what made me hurry along the streets was my desire to be here: not on the

balcony where my father sits but in the room—this room—
and at its window—this window that I know will be—at this
particular moment—closed, giving an impression of emptiness behind it. But I will be here waiting. I remove my shoes
slowly; my feet ache from their long imprisonment. I do it
slowly because I am trying to make the time pass. Surely I
will not have to wait long. I stand up, refreshing my bare feet
on the cool tiles. This is another way of making the time pass,
this interval of waiting. I am also forcing it to pass when I
return to where my father sits. He must wake up now, I tell
myself; it's better for him, when I bring him his food, to have
come up at least partly from the crevasse into which his napping has dropped him.

XXXI

NOT ONLY WERE THE TWO houses empty for us, but also the stairs between them and likewise the stairs below, all the way to the building's entryway. The entire building had emptied out for us. If I could take a single step forward, then we could behave as if it were a single dwelling or a vast hiding place among whose niches we could range, loitering in its darkest and narrowest spots: on the stairs, on the little landing that leads directly to their front door, which we would keep open so that even more darkness could pour in to envelop us in our concealment. Or at the threshold to their home, because even if we were hiding there it would look as though we were guarding the emptiness of the building from the echo of feet arriving suddenly at the bottom of the stairs. Or in this room of mine whose window and door I would close to turn it into a smaller space. Or even at the top of the stairs above me, where no one has gone since who knows when.

There at the very top of the stairs sits a rooftop room, and if we were there it would be like being inside a tall chest. It would enclose us together, close to each other, touching each other or, rather, pressing against each other, since the narrowness of the room would not allow for any space between us. We would not need to speak, voices rising above the sound of our breathing, which we're unaware of at first, though we become slowly aware of how strong and loud it is. We'll be encased in darkness, and also in the air of the ancient, which makes things darker. An old gloom that brings our faces closer together, no longer two separate faces, each one furtively slipping out through its own window to be dispersed in the wide world stretching out across the expanse of sand. Being so near to each other will bring us together, there in the rooftop room that's so much like a tall, narrow box. We will hear only our breaths rising, dusty and chasing each other, as if hurrying us along to the place where we'll do something to release them, loud and panting. She will be close to me there, in the cramped, dark room. I will not even need to come any closer when her breast emerges, tinted deeper by the darkness, from the blouse whose buttons she has undone. Her breast will be close to me as it comes out into the darkness, where it gleams with its own light even as the darkness shadows it. It will emerge held in her hand, which has brought it out; and she will go on holding it as if to bring it closer to me. To me—and, so near, I will be able to breathe in its fragrance, which will be no different from its taste when I take the nipple between my lips.

The little room over the stairs will bring us together, touching each other or pressed together hearing the sounds of our breathing, loud and insistent as if urging us on. Her legs will be trying to escape toward the tiny narrow door we have closed. But she will know, when I grip her leg to flex it, that I want her foot, which is hidden too. When I squeeze its toes together in my little hand, it's as if I am hiding her foot again, or covering it up so that I can reveal it again, lifting my hand from it. Her toes: my hand is not big enough to cover them, so I move it among them, grasping one after another until I reach her big toe which, as I enclose it, I can feel stands apart, erect with the desire in her body concentrated there, a taut and waiting nerve.

Separate and firm—and I will hold it in my grip as if I want to feel the tension there and at the same time quiet and dispel it. We are concealed there, not only from the woman and my mother but also from the vast space of the two homes that we have left empty. There, in the dark and ancient space, I will feel her tension and then I'll know, holding it in my grip, where that tension began in order to reach its end here in her big toe. I'll be able to relax it, because the tension and the hardness inside of her pain me. I'll turn toward her, to the center of her, where all begins. And from there I will see her face too, thrown back and submerged in an ecstasy that seems to be hers alone. She distances herself, closing her eyes and moving her lips as if whispering to herself; whispering things that cannot be heard.

XXXII

THEIR WORK PRODUCED NOTHING VISIBLE, there
on the land of the old city, until after my father died. Then
two buildings appeared, or their skeletons did, like one dark,
massed shadow. They rose suddenly, just like that, as if they
had been built horizontally on the ground and then raised
up with ropes or heavy machines to suddenly stand erect, two
complete skeletons. In the days following his death I would
stand in his place, where he used to sit, and stare at the vast
empty space to see if they had begun anything there. I was
doing it for his sake, as if—for his sake—to keep watch over
the one thing that had most clearly occupied him as he wondered how it would all be after his death.

I was doing it for him, and in his way. He believed that
what he had left behind him would become real and tangible
and unmovable despite his death. I was doing this in the way
he would have done. To know what that was, I needed only to
re-create his prolonged patience: during that lingering period
he had never stopped saying, Look, do you see anything?

Look, look—have they started anything?

In his hours on the balcony, when he was still capable
of speaking, he would think of his shop, even if it sat empty,
without him, as if he were carefully preserving a future for it

that would be his even if it lacked his living presence. When I stand here on the balcony where he sat, looking at the whole sweeping aspect that would have lain to his left, I am doing it for his sake and in his way: I take the care he took, I continue it, to know where they have gotten to now, as if for the sake of making certain that someone remains alert to what is going on over there.

They are two buildings that rose suddenly, towering and so close together that from the distance between us I think they look slightly bowed, seeming to lean in toward each other. So—they did begin the work. I didn't know whether it was the slow pace of their work that had caused the delay. On the balcony from which I could see the two buildings, I said to myself that—now they had begun—I could ignore them. I would not need to follow what they were doing every day, as if, in checking to see whether indeed a building or two had gone up, I then needed to point them out to someone nearby, waving my hand in their direction just as my father used to do to guide us to his shop.

Leaving the balcony I stared at the floor as if I had to make certain that nothing had been left there. There was no need now for me to leave the door open. I would be careful not to come out here very often; I would only come out here to flash a quick glance over there to see whether they were getting on with what they had begun. That's all, nothing more, and then I would leave the balcony, looking around to check that nothing had been left on the floor. The chair on which my father sat seemed weighted down by all his years of occupying it. I carried it into his room the day after his burial and set it between the bed and the wardrobe, facing the door, as if it was awaiting someone who would come to sit there and had positioned itself to be ready, there, facing the door whenever it might be opened. It didn't look right there. Set down in there with its two large cushions that had supported my father's bottom and back, it gave the room a look of finality, as though it were about to be closed forever; or as if it were now ready to receive whatever other furnishings the house was ready to throw out.

Instead, I would go to those who bought old things, whom I had come to know. The sum I got from selling my books I spent on burying my father, since I had to pay people even to lift the bier onto their shoulders to hoist it into the car that—like the truck that had come to take away my books— turned its open rear end to face the building's entryway. On my way back, as I walked toward a home where I knew I would confront the emptiness alone, the thought came to me that he had killed himself slowly this way to give me the time I needed to arrange the affairs of death—and also to figure out how to manage my life without him.

It seemed to me he had appointed the time of his own death, setting a predetermined date so I could prepare for it before it happened. For they did take all the money I had collected from selling my books. They finished their work without needing anything further, even my presence among them. When they lowered him into his grave it seemed as though they were merely returning something to its own berth that had simply waited, empty, for him. They even brought me the flowers I must put over his grave. And before I left, before they had collected their tools and belongings, they showed me how to get to my father's grave, how I could guide myself to him among the many tombs arranged in squares separated by corridors and branching passageways. One of them accompanied me out to help me learn the route so that I could return by myself. My mother had stayed at a distance with the woman, as if they were waiting for the surroundings to empty out so that they could approach the grave. From there I walked toward the home I would enter alone. Now it was mine, since my mother had let go of most of her part. The only share she had had in it, in the time before my father's death, was sleeping and waking there, and then standing in the kitchen for a few moments to add something new to yesterday's cooking. From now on I would take a part of that remaining share. I would cook my own food with my own hands.

This is my home: I will not simply live here; I will live off this house. I will eat from it. I returned my father's chair to his room and shut the door on it and its two cushions because of how much they reminded me of him, keeping him near as though he were still alive. I put the chair in there to stay, in the narrow space between the wardrobe and the bed, facing the door and awaiting the traces of my father's soul. But I will not leave it, along with the room's other furnishings, to grow ancient behind the closed door, wearing out where they sit. Those who brought the truck to take my books will come again, bringing their truck again too, to lift everything from the tile flooring, which will look naked when they have gone. I will close the door on the tiles and turn away, and I will not open the door again. Thus I will have excluded one part of this house, leaving it closer to the empty space and air outside than it is to the interior I occupy.

This house of mine: I will live here and it will feed me, too. Its old worn furniture will not bring much money, but I won't eat much, only the amount of food equal to its value. As they are miserly about what they pay for what they take, so I will be miserly with what I eat. The furniture that my father was waiting to take back to the old city will now go, truckload after truckload, to where my father hated even to buy meat and vegetables for us. Like ants, he would snap, speaking of those who had gone on with their lives there. He would narrow the space between his two fingers until it was as slight as the body of an ant, and then he would let his fingers scurry from one side to the other, changing direction. Like ants, he would say as his ant scampered across to where he planted his two fingers. They had planted themselves there, to go on with the rest of their lives. Someone who had had a roomy shop in the old city consented over here to cram his merchandise into the entryway of a building or under its stairs. They had accepted it so that they could resume business, hoping it would be temporary. And here I am sending our home's furniture there, truckload after truckload. My mother has already gone, and the woman has gone with her; they delayed going there, but finally they did it. As for the one for whom I stand leaning on the windowsill, waiting for her to appear from the room beneath me, she will not be long to go either. She is getting ready for it. I know it from her face. Whenever she lifts it to me I can see it growing older, only to change, no longer that face I've grown accustomed to from the sight of her in her window and what I can see of her room just inside it. Every time her face is lifted to me I can see the other look that lurks behind the look she raises to me. That other look, the sly and expectant one, can overpower the first look whenever she decides she wants it to.

I know she will go, too. I know that no one will be left in the building but me. Waiting for that, I will go on standing here at the window, for her. I will not be content simply to expel the second look from her eyes, which makes them gleam with expectation. No, I will bring back that face of hers, small and young, its cheeks not yet full or shaped into hardness, and no tiny hairs over the lip giving that toughness an even stranger glint. I will go on seeing her as young, the way I love her, giving the lie to what I see now and ridding her of it by merely turning away from the window and moving my face further back from hers. It will be like sketching her face anew, bringing her back, but in contrast to what I see before I turn to face the interior of my room.

But I know all the while that I will not be able to keep the two faces battling each other forever, one eliminating the other and taking its place. It will not be long before the two faces depart, each to go their own way. And when this time arrives, either I will have to close my window at last or I will wait for her to leave for the new city, where I expect she has been preparing herself to live.

XXXIII

THE TRUCK THAT HAD LET out that screech on the sand track carried off the contents of my father's room. The two men who had come with it last time to take my books took apart the wardrobe so that they could carry it. They added what they brought down to the heap they had already piled up in the truck. Over the bed that they carried down in three pieces they laid the thin old mattress, slept on for so many years, rolled up and bound with thin rope. Next to it were placed my father's clothes, rolled up in a sheet that the men took from among the belongings in his wardrobe. As for his chair, from which the two cushions had been detached, it was placed on the very top of the heap, perching there conspicuously even if its four legs sank into the belongings piled beneath it.

After the two men had gone I closed the door to the room on the thick sweepings of dust that the pieces of absent furniture had left behind. I saw no use in sweeping it, since no one would open the room. No one had any business there. The balcony door, too, I could leave shut, since I had familiarized myself with the rhythm of their work as they put up scattered buildings along the the curving edge of ringed-in city. In his final days my father was not only concluding his life slowly; he was at the end of the traces that would remain after him, sitting there at the balcony wall or in his room that he had abandoned except for sleep. And then, I thought, he had moved there, to lie in his grave, just as a man changes where he sits or sleeps. I must not forget the way to his grave. If that were to happen it would be as if I had left him without anyone who knows him, there among the graves that grow more and more numerous as more squares are laid out, creating new paths between them. I must not lose the way to him, even if it means going there very often, to make sure that the grave is still in its place—the place I know. I will go on doing that, for myself, because there is no one to say to me, when I lose the way, Come—the grave is over here! I do it for myself alone. I am behaving as my father did with his shop, believing I am taking some kind of action if I go on visiting a grave. I see it as calming the dead soul of my father, bringing it helpful messages that give it companionship and comfort.

I must be careful not to lose his grave—even if it does lie there, in the new city that I don't like, as he did not either . In any case it is a fixed point where something of him remains. In the house here—in this building that rises on the sand like a thick, short tower—I will go on reducing and compressing what is around me. Having closed up my father's room, I don't know what I will sell when the tiny sum I received last time runs out. I figure next time I'll sell sundry things that they'll pick out from the furnishings throughout the apartment. I will do it this way for the sake of leaving the sitting room as it is, though I don't need it as a sitting room, and likewise to preserve the dining room even though I can eat my food without this room remaining as a dining room.

I sell things that they carry off from among the furniture and the entire apartment begins to diminish. When my mother comes through the front doorway heading for her room, she will not look for very long at the empty place where the flower vase was, or that held the little bedside table with its woodcut patterns. If and when she passes through, all she's thinking about is whatever it is she came to pick up. Anyway, she will match the rhythm of this emptying house by visiting less often and staying for ever shorter periods.

Yes, this house will empty of its furnishings and of her at the same gradual rate. Moreover, she has already made sure of that. Her room—and the way to her room—are still completely furnished, while she has left them so far behind in her own departures. I have a lot to sell before I reach that race, when we will compete, when I will be matching her pace for pace. First I will sell the little things, those strewn among the tables and the sofas, items that can be lifted with one hand, or even both but without needing ropes to tie them up. In the next round, they will take things that require dislodging, and that require opening the fixed half of the outside door to get them out.

This is my house, and I will stay here, eating from its belongings as I sell them off. Of all its windows the only one I will open is the one in my room that looks down on her, there below. And I will open the door to the room that my family said was my room though I never slept in it. From there, from the window that looks down onto the sand track, I will see her when she begins to go out, her too, walking slowly and moving her buttocks, on her arm the bag in which she has put things women use to make themselves prettier. She has already begun to prepare for it, in the apartment where she spends her time alone. She still goes over to the window but she does it at times I cannot predict; and every time she twists her body outward to see me, the gaze she lifts to me is too

221

strong to be meant for me. It's as if I am one object among many that happen to fall into the space she sees, or as if when she looks she does not give much of her mind or attention to what she's seeing. I am sure of this when she retreats from the window abruptly to head toward something inside that she has been thinking about.

I move between the two windows so that I can see her here and then see her leaving from over there. I know it will not be long before she begins to go out, leaving the home below me empty. Yet I will not stop moving between the two windows, so that I can see her coming when she returns. Then I'll head to the other window. I know I will go on doing it as long as she is still coming back from these departures of hers.

She will go out, moving her buttocks slowly as she walks, on her arm the little bag that will take her even further away from me. She will empty the entire building for me. I will no longer hear any sounds rising, except for the few I make as I pace among the rooms with their open doors, sounds that will echo ever louder and longer as the house empties of the remaining furniture that waits inside.